Aliens from Flinduvia want our ghosts for ammunition!

"Are we going to go there?" I asked nervously. I was beginning to wonder if Sarah and I would ever get home.

"I have not yet decided whether we should go to Flinduvia. That had been my initial intent," said the Wentar, "but we also need to take a warning back to Earth."

"I don't get it," said Sarah. "Who would you take the message to? The FBI? The president?"

"Even if they believed us, they wouldn't know what to do," said the Wentar. "No, we need to get our warning to those most in peril."

He took a deep breath. "We need to warn the dead."

Look for these other Bruce Coville titles from Scholastic:

Bruce Coville's Book of Monsters
Bruce Coville's Book of Aliens
Bruce Coville's Book of Ghosts
Bruce Coville's Book of Nightmares
Bruce Coville's Book of Spine Tinglers
Bruce Coville's Book of Magic
Bruce Coville's Book of Monsters II
Bruce Coville's Book of Aliens II

and coming soon:

Bruce Coville's Book of Nightmares II (March 1997)
Bruce Coville's Book of Spine Tinglers II (May 1997)
Bruce Coville's Book of Magic II (July 1997)

BRUCE COVILLE'S BOOK OF

Compiled and edited by
Bruce Coville

Assisted by
Lisa Meltzer

Illustrated by
John Pierard

A GLC Book

SCHOLASTIC INC.
New York Toronto London Auckland Sydney

For all those who have gone before.

ISBN: 0-590-85294-9

12 11 10 9 8 7 6 5 4 3 2 1 7 8 9/9 0 2/0

Printed in the U.S.A. 40

First Scholastic printing, January 1997

CONTENTS

Contents

INTRODUCTION: A FAINT PRESENCE, A COLD TOUCH

Some think that the dead are hungry for the living, that they crave our vitality, are jealous of our juice.

That may be true. But is it not equally true that the living are hungry for the dead? Do we not haunt them, eager for their stories, seeking their blessing, their forgiveness, their knowledge of what lies beyond?

Why won't we let them rest? I mean, if we are really so afraid of ghosts, why are we so attracted to haunted houses, so drawn to graveyards, so curious about the places where Death has paid a recent visit?

Partly, I suppose, it's because they seem so real to us. I mean, surely you've sensed it, one time or another—the lingering presence, the unexplained coldness, the sourceless sound that tells you the world, for a moment, is not as we think it should be.

That the normal rules have been abandoned.

That the dead are visiting the living.

And with that sense comes a shudder of fear, terror at the thought of their cold touch, their faint presence.

Well, you might as well get used to it. Because the way I figure it, there are more ghosts every day. The future may not be getting smaller, but the past is definitely getting bigger. Each time the sun sets, another day is added to the past. Which means that every day the world has more wrongs left unrighted, more hearts left broken, more connections missed, hurts unhealed, sins (both small and large) left unrepented and unforgiven.

In short, every time the sun sets, it leaves behind more reasons for a place, or person, or thing to be *haunted;* more ghosts with stories that need to be told.

Which is exactly what waits for you in these pages: A collection of tales in which someone or some*thing* has unfinished business that keeps it tied to this earthly plane rather than moving on to . . . well, to whatever it is that comes next.

So come along, gentle reader. You know you're curious. Why not let our cold friends take you by the hand and tell you their stories?

Try not to fear their touch.

After all—sooner or later, we all have to learn what they already know. . . .

A TRIP TO THE LAND OF THE DEAD

(Part 3 of "The Monsters of Morley Manor")

Bruce Coville

What has happened so far:

You think you've got troubles? How would you like to be me, Anthony Walker? Along with my little sister, Sarah, I went to a house sale at Morley Manor after Old Man Morley died. (At least, everyone thought he was dead.) Sarah found a neat wooden box in the house's library, which I decided to buy.

Who would have guessed that the five monster figurines I found inside weren't toys, but *real* monsters who had been shrunk and put

under a spell that made them seem frozen? But after my mother's monkey splashed water on one of them, it began to flex its tiny fist. So Sarah and I decided to thaw them out. Soon we had five cranky little monsters insisting on being taken back to the old house so they could get big again.

No sooner had we done *that* than an old friend of one of the monsters, a strange being called the Wentar of Ardis, showed up and whisked us through a "Starry Door" to a strange planet where we learned that a group of aliens was planning to invade earth. What they were after was very surprising. . . .

I. Where Do the Dead Live?

Gaspar leaned close to the frog creature. "What do you mean, the Flinduvians want our ghosts for ammunition?"

Unk swallowed hard, making a deep, ribbity sound. "I do not know all the details, only what I overheard. The spirits of your dead have unusually powerful energy. The Flinduvians want to use them in a new weapon they have invented."

"That is the most immoral thing I have ever heard," said Gaspar. His long tongue flicked angrily from between his big lizardy jaws.

I had to agree. Killing the part of a person that

lives on beyond death sounded worse than murder to me. Or maybe it wouldn't kill them. With something like this, who could tell? Whatever it would do, it didn't sound good.

"How did you overhear this?" asked the Wentar. "What is your connection with the Flinduvians?"

"I am one of their primary contacts for this planet."

"Does our mother know this?" asked Chuck. He sounded shocked.

"No," replied Unk, in a kind of moan.

I could see why he would moan if he thought this would make his mother unhappy, since she was the size of a small office building. Being on momma's bad side was definitely a bad idea for these frog-critters.

"What else do you know of their plans?" asked the Wentar.

"Nothing!" said Unk. His voice sounded desperate. Finally the Wentar told us to let him up—which broke the hypnotic spell that we had him under.

"All right," said the Wentar. "I want you to take us to the Starry Door that leads to Flinduvia."

"Are we going to go there?" I asked nervously. I was beginning to wonder if Sarah and I would ever get home.

My nervousness was nothing compared to

Unk's reaction. "I can't!" he gasped, his big eyes goggling.

"Silence!" said the Wentar. Turning back to me, he said, "I have not yet decided whether we should go to Flinduvia. That had been my initial intent, since I need to see if we can regain Martin. Even if we decide against it, I need to see the door, since I can gather some important information from it. But we also need to take a warning back to Earth."

"Perhaps we should split up," suggested Gaspar.

"Vat a good idea," said Darlene. "Ve should not involve the children in this anyway."

Part of me was offended. Part of me was going, *Darn right! Get us out of here!*

The Wentar shook his head. "Andrew and Sarah are part of this already. Since the Flinduvians are aware of them, sending them back will not necessarily mean they are safe. The primary reason to split up would be to carry the message back at once."

"I don't get it," said Sarah. "Who would you take the message to? The FBI? The president?"

Gaspar laughed. "It's unlikely they would believe us, even if we could actually reach them."

"I dunno," I said. "If the president got a look at you guys, he'd have to believe almost anything." Then I blushed, wondering if I had said something that would offend them.

"Even if they believed you, they wouldn't know what to do," said the Wentar. "No, we need to get our warning to those most in peril."

"What do you mean?" asked Albert.

The Wentar took a deep breath. "We need to warn the dead."

Bob, the weredog, began to howl.

"How the heck do we do *that?*" I asked nervously.

"Someone has to make a trip to the Land of the Dead," said the Wentar with a shrug.

"That sounds pretty scary," whispered Sarah.

"Ssshe sssspeaks ssssooth," hissed the snakes on Marie's head. I could tell from the way they were writhing that she was upset.

"I don't even understand what it means," I said. "What's the Land of the Dead? Where is it?"

The Wentar looked very serious. Actually, with his long face and mournful eyes, he always looked serious. But now he looked even more so.

"It is a world between life and death," he whispered. "A place where the lost and the rebellious, the stubborn and the misguided wait, and plan, and grieve, and mourn. It is not the right place for them to be. The dead should move on to what is next. But not everyone is ready to let go of the previous stage of life. Sometimes it is pain that holds them, or anger, or unfinished business of one sort or another. Sometimes it is simply that they cannot let go of those they love. Sometimes, very rarely, it is joy that holds them. It is a realm of great souls and small, a place that is not a place. Grief runs there like flowing water. Solace, too, though most ignore it. Some souls never see this place. Some stay no more than a day. But others—stubborn, or blind, or in deeper pain than most—may remain for centuries."

I felt a coldness in my blood as he spoke, a chill that lingered in my spine.

"How do you get there?" asked Sarah in a hushed voice.

"The easiest way is to die," said the Wentar.

When he saw the look on our faces he began to chuckle. "You needn't worry! Just because it is the easiest way does not mean that it is the only way, or even the best. The most likely avenue is actually through a connection. Do any of you know someone who has died lately?"

"Ve haf been locked in a box for the last fifty years," pointed out Darlene. "I suspect *most* of the people ve used to know haf died. But who can guess *ven* they did it?"

"Of coursse, there wassss Martin," hissed Marie's snakes.

"But he was not the real Martin," pointed out Albert.

"Real or not, it doesn't make any difference," said the Wentar. "Remember, the clone of your brother did not die, it was taken back to Flinduvia, and replaced with a replica that had never actually been alive to begin with."

"What about you two?" asked Albert, turning toward Sarah and me.

"There was Grampa Walker," said Sarah slowly.

I didn't say anything; couldn't get the words past the lump in my throat.

"When did he die?" asked the Wentar. To my surprise, his voice was sympathetic.

"About three months ago," said Sarah. Her voice trembled a little.

"Is it likely that he would be the sort not to move on?" asked Gaspar.

"Well, he *was* stubborn," I said.

"And he might be waiting for Gramma," added Sarah.

"Then he may be our best ticket," said the Wentar.

I didn't particularly like the idea of my grandfather as a "ticket" to the land of the dead. But I liked the idea of his soul being used for ammunition by some bizarre alien race even less. Grampa Walker had been—well, I loved him a lot. I didn't sleep very well for the first month after he died. And I had cried a lot. I had one of his old pipes in my sock drawer.

Sometimes I took it out and smelled it, just to remember him better.

"Are you willing to do this?" asked the Wentar, looking at Sarah and me.

I felt her hand reach out and take mine. Normally, I would have yanked it away. But we were in too deep for that that kind of stuff now. I looked at her. Her eyes were wide and frightened. I raised an eyebrow. She gave me just the slightest nod.

I turned to the Wentar.

"We'll do it."

II. "What Will We Tell Gramma?"

The plan we finally decided on was simple. The Wentar, Darlene and Albert would go with Unk to examine the Flinduvian Door. If the Wentar decided it was a good idea, they would then go through it and search for Martin. If not, they would meet us back at Morley Manor as soon as possible.

Meanwhile Chuck, the friendly frog-critter, would lead the rest of us to the Starry Door that connected to Earth. Once we were home, Gaspar would try to get us to the land of the dead, so we could bring our warning.

"What about the Flinduvians who were chasing us when we left?" asked Sarah.

It was exactly the sort of sensible thing I could count on her to think of.

"They should have left by now," said the Wentar. "Patience is not one of their virtues. However if they are still there, you can use this to buy yourself some time. Just fling it to the floor, and it will create an effective . . . distraction."

As he spoke, he pressed something into Gaspar's hand. The lizard-headed scientist slipped it into his pocket. Then he and the Wentar went off to have a conversation about how, exactly, we were supposed to get to the land of the dead.

Once that was over, we said our good-byes. They didn't take long, but they were intense, since we all knew it was possible that we might not meet again. Gaspar and Darlene hugged for a long time. "Be careful, little sister," he whispered fiercely. Then he let her go.

I looked at my own little sister. I realized that even though Sarah bugged the daylights out of me, I would kill to keep her safe. And I realized something else, too: for all that the monsters looked so horrible, and acted fairly strange, their feelings were, in many ways, not that different from ours.

The Wentar's group started out first. We watched them go until they were nearly out of sight. Then we turned and started across the springy grass. The purple sky arched above us, and the air smelled clean and spicy. I think that smell may have been the most alien thing of all. It wasn't bad. In fact, I kind of liked it. But it was so different from the air I was used to that, more than the purple sky or the weird flowers or the broccoli-like grass, it made me know I was a long way from home.

I wondered what time it was back on Earth. How long had we been gone? The Wentar had said that time operated differently on different worlds. Had it only been a few minutes—or would we get home to find that we had been gone for days, or even years?

We had been so busy trying to survive that I hadn't really thought about these things. Now I couldn't get them out of my head. Was Gramma Walker still sleeping soundly in our house? Or had she woken to find us gone? Was she even now panicking, terrified, calling our parents to come home from their florist's conference?

"We'd better hurry," I said.

Gaspar nodded. "A great deal depends on what we do next."

I wondered how we were going to explain that to Gramma.

It was only about a fifteen-minute walk back to the place where we had stepped out of the Starry Door, though it seemed to take much longer. Bob the weredog kept running ahead of us and then bounding back. Marie tried to get him to settle down, without much success.

"Sssseee what I musssst live with?" hissed the snakes that writhed around her head.

Finally we reached the spot where the door was supposed to be. Only when we got there, the door itself was nowhere to be seen.

"What happened to it?" I cried, afraid we were going to be stuck in this weird world forever.

"Doors such as this one are not constantly open," said Gaspar gently. "Think of the trouble it would cause if they were! Not only would people be hopping from planet to planet all the time, which would be bad enough, but all sorts of wildlife might wander through as well. That could really create chaos!"

Marie began to laugh, and her snakes made a kind of sporadic hissing that I realized was the snake version of laughing.

"What's so funny?" I asked.

"I wassss thinking of what people on Earth would sssay if they could ssseee my petsss on Zentarazzzzna."

"What is Zentarazna?" asked Sarah. "Darlene mentioned it once before."

"It issss the plassss we would rather be," she answered, and that was all she would say about it, even though Sarah tried to ask her some more questions while we waited for Gaspar and

Chuck to get the door open. I sat on the grass and watched. It was kind of interesting to see how they did it. But I'm not supposed to talk about it.

Watching the door actually open was very weird. First there was nothing but air in front of us. Then, slowly, this shimmering oval began to appear.

It seemed like it took forever for it to finish taking shape, though really it was only about ten minutes. The thing was, once it *was* ready, I sort of wished it wasn't. I didn't know if I was ready to go back yet.

Actually, it wasn't going back that worried me. It was what we had to do when we got there.

The purple sky had grown dark above us. We said farewell to Chuck. I looked around, thinking how strange it all was, and wondering if I would ever again have a chance to go to another planet. Then we stepped into the Starry Door.

Again I felt that weird tingle, as if I were being stung by a thousand bees and kissed by a thousand butterflies all at the same time.

My body was still tingling when I realized I was standing back in the upstairs hallway of Morley Manor—the hall that stretched on long past where the house itself should end.

"Home," said Gaspar.

"For you," I muttered.

"What time do you think it is?" asked Sarah.

I shrugged. None of us were wearing watches. There were no clocks left in the house, since they had all been sold along with the rest of the furniture. And from where we were standing, you couldn't even tell if it was dark or light outside.

"Come on," said Gaspar. "If we go outdoors we can at least get a rough idea of the time—though we won't necessarily know what day it is."

We followed him back along the corridor, then down the stairs. I kept looking over my shoulder, wondering if the Flinduvians were waiting to leap out and ambush us.

No sign of them.

We stepped outside and Gaspar scanned the sky. "I'd guess it's about four in the morning," he said. "That makes things a little tricky, since we need to make the crossing to the Land of the Dead at midnight."

"There's a paper box two blocks up," said Sarah. "We can check the date there."

Gaspar glanced around. "I am not comfortable going that far away. I would . . . rather not be seen."

I hadn't thought about that until now. When we had brought the monsters back to Morley Manor, they had been only five inches high, so it had been no problem to hide them. But at full size, Gaspar was well over six feet—not to mention that his lizard head was at least two feet long.

"I'll check it," said Sarah. "Be right back."

"I'll go with you," I said.

"Wait!" said Gaspar. But it was too late. We were on our way. I think he was nervous that we might run off on him. The truth was simpler. I was still worried about the Flinduvians, and I didn't want Sarah to run into them on her own. What good I could have done by being with her I couldn't say. In some ways, it was a stupid thing to do. But in my heart, it felt right.

"Uh-oh," I said, when I saw the paper box. "We've been gone a whole day!"

Sarah looked at the newspaper for a moment, then began to laugh. "No we haven't!"

"But it says Monday. It was Sunday night when we went into Morley Manor."

"And after midnight it was Monday morning," said Sarah, as if she was explaining something to a moron. "This is the morning paper. They start putting them out at about four or so."

How did she know this kind of stuff?

"All right, let's go back and tell Gaspar the good news," I said, feeling kind of grumpy.

He was standing on the walk just inside the large gate, out of sight from anyone who might happen by—which wasn't likely, considering the location. His worried look changed when he saw us returning.

"Everything's fine," I said. "It's Monday morning, just like it should be, and . . . holy mackerel, I forgot!"

III. The Original Package!

"What?" asked Sarah and Gaspar together. "What is it?"

"Monday morning," I said, my voice weak. "They're going to start tearing this place down today!"

"They can't do that!" said Gaspar indignantly.

"I told you they were going to," I pointed out.

Of course, that had been five hours ago. A lot had happened since then, including being chased by horrible aliens, making a trip to another planet, and finding out that the very souls of our dead were in danger.

"We will have to take quick action," said Gaspar. He looked from side to side, almost as if hoping to find someone to help him. His shoulders slumped. We were on our own.

"All right, here's what we have to do," he said at last. "Come back inside with me. I will need your help in returning to my human shape."

"You can do that whenever you want?" I asked, startled by the idea.

"Not easily," said Gaspar.

"Do you mind telling us how you got this way?" asked Sarah.

"Not at all, when I have time. Right now we have to get this done, and then get you home. Actually, if we turn me back to human form, I can escort you home more easily. Come on."

When we went inside, Gaspar announced that Marie should transform herself as well.

She didn't like the idea. And her snakes liked it even less. They set up a horrible hissing and fizzing.

"We really have no choice," said Gaspar urgently.

"What about Bob?" I asked, gesturing toward the weredog.

"There's nothing we can do about him now," said Gaspar. "His transformation was of a different sort than ours."

He led the way upstairs to his laboratory. For a moment I was worried that the Flinduvians might have smashed it in a fit of spite, but fortunately it was still intact. I was glad. I thought the combination of lab stuff and magic stuff was major cool. It would have been sad to see it busted up.

The green jewel called the Heart of Wentar that provided power for the whole operation still rested in the control box. Gaspar gave Sarah and me our instructions. Then he and Marie went to stand on two of the platforms at the far side of the laboratory. At Gaspar's nod, I pulled a lever. A pair of glass chambers descended from the ceiling. Marie's snakes started going wild, thrashing and tying themselves in knots.

Gaspar nodded again, and Sarah and I set to work, pulling levers and shifting dials. A fantastic humming filled the room, getting louder and louder. Sparks crackled through the glass chambers, which began to fill with green mist. Electricity—or maybe some other kind of power I don't know about—began to skitter over the surface of the chambers. Gaspar screamed.

"We've got to turn it off!" said Sarah.

"No! He told us that might happen."

He screamed again.

"I can't stand it!" cried Sarah. "Turn it off, Anthony!"

She lunged for the main lever. I caught her just in time. "Don't!" I said urgently. "If we turn it off now, Gaspar and Marie might be caught halfway between human and monster!"

Gaspar screamed again. This time he was joined by Marie, whose high-pitched shriek seemed to wind around his, spiraling upward. I felt as if someone was scraping shards of glass down a blackboard.

"Stop it!" screamed Sarah, struggling to escape my grasp.

She may be nicer than I am, but sometimes nice isn't the answer. I held on to her with all my might. It wasn't easy, because I couldn't stand the screams either. I hoped I was making the right choice. Finally I heard three loud snaps, just as Gaspar had said we would, and the mist in the chambers turned purple.

"There!" I said, letting go of Sarah. "Now we can turn it off."

Her face was streaked with tears. "I hate you!" she hissed.

Ignoring her, I pulled the lever that would lift the chambers.

Coughing and choking, Gaspar and Marie stepped out.

They were completely human looking. In fact, they were gorgeous, like movie stars.

"Holy mackerel!" cried Sarah. Then, turning toward me, she muttered, "Sorry, Anthony."

"Don't worry about it, kid," I replied softly. "When you're big like me, you'll know better."

She kicked me. I would have been mad, but I figured I deserved it. Besides, it was worth it.

Gaspar stretched and rubbed his arms, then shook his head like a dog that just climbed out of the water. Marie reached up and touched her own head, then made a terrible face. "How boring!" she muttered, as she ran her hands through her tangled black hair. It was thick and glossy.

Bob took one look at the two of them and began to howl.

"So—now what do we do?" I asked.

"Change our clothes," said Marie decisively. It was funny to hear her speak in her own voice. Without any hissing. She was wearing a kind of white shroud, and while it looked pretty good on her, all things considered, she sure couldn't go out that way without attracting attention.

"Good idea," said Gaspar.

"Good idea, but not much chance," said Sarah.

"Why not?" asked Marie.

"Well, aside from the fact that any clothes you had would be fifty years out of style now, I doubt there are any here. Remember, they had a sale to clear the place out before the wreckers came."

"Can you help us?" asked Gaspar desperately. "I have to get to a lawyer immediately."

Sarah glanced at me. "Do you suppose they could wear Mom and Dad's clothes?"

I didn't think Mom and Dad would be particularly pleased by the idea. On the other hand, we were in so far at this point that I figured a little thing like that shouldn't slow us down. "Hard to say. I think Gaspar is a little taller than Dad. Might work. I don't know about Marie and Mom."

"Let's go," said Gaspar.

"What about Bob?" I asked.

Gaspar looked at Bob. The weredog began to whine.

"We'd better take him with us," said Gaspar. "If anyone comes along, we'll try to hide him."

As it turned out, it wasn't necessary. When we went outside a pale light was creeping across the sky. Bob began to bark. Then he flopped onto his side and kicked, the way dogs do when they're dreaming. Then he rolled over and over.

In a few moments, he was a floppy-eared cocker spaniel, panting and wagging his tail.

"That is too weird," said Sarah.

"What a good dog," said Marie, patting Bob's head.

"Come on," said Gaspar. "We have to hurry."

Easy for him to say. He wasn't going to have to explain all this to his grandmother.

We slipped into the house. Gramma was still asleep, though how long that would last, I wasn't certain. We weren't likely to wake her with our noise—she was pretty deaf. But she was also an early riser.

I didn't want to think about rising. I didn't

want to think at all. I wanted to sleep. "I don't think I've ever been so tired in my entire life," I muttered—which made sense, when you considered what had been going on.

"Help us find something to wear," said Gaspar urgently.

Sarah led the way to our parents' bedroom. Even though I didn't think Gramma would hear us, we moved quietly.

It took about a half an hour, and a few pins, but we finally got Gaspar and Marie looking pretty acceptable.

"Now what?" I asked.

"Now I go wake up some poor lawyer and try to save the house," said Gaspar. "In the meantime, you two get some rest. Tonight, we have to make a trip to the land of the dead."

IV. The Missing Link

Despite the fact that I was exhausted, my mind was in such a whirl that I didn't know if I would be able to sleep or not. I didn't need to worry. The minute I hit the sheets I fell into a sleep so deep it was like being dead.

I didn't wake up until noon.

When I staggered out to the kitchen, Gramma was standing at the counter, kneading some bread dough. Mr. Perkins, my mother's monkey, was sitting on his perch, eating an apple.

It all looked so normal that I began to wonder if everything that had happened last night was some sort of weird dream after all.

Gramma turned up her hearing aid when she saw me. "Good morning, slugabed. What did you two do last night, sneak out and watch TV after I had gone to sleep?"

"Something like that," I said with a yawn. "Is Sarah up?"

"She's in the bathroom. Why don't you pour yourself a bowl of cereal."

That sounded like a good idea. I had been so tired when we got in that I forgot I was also starving.

Mr. Perkins hissed at me as I went to the cupboard. It made me think of Marie. I wondered how she and Gaspar were making out with their mission to save Morley Manor.

Before I could worry about it too much, there was a knock at the door. Gramma didn't hear it, of course, but when I went to get it she noticed, and said, "I'll get that, Anthony. You eat."

While she was gone, Sarah came back to the kitchen. I was considering asking her if last night had really happened when Gramma came back, too. She had a weird look on her face.

Marie and Gaspar were with her, Bob trotting alongside them.

"These people say they're friends of yours," said Gramma, looking a little puzzled. (It may seem strange to some of you that she would let them in, but you have to remember that in Owl's Roost, Nebraska, people still leave their doors unlocked at night. We are not what you would call the crime capital of the world.)

"How did you make out?" I asked, jumping to my feet.

Gaspar smiled. "We got a temporary injunction to stop the demolition. Morley Manor still stands."

"Gracious!" said Gramma. "What do you have to do with Morley Manor?"

Then she narrowed her eyes.

"Gaspar?" she asked.

He looked at her curiously.

She clutched her heart. "Gaspar!" she said accusingly.

He looked at her again, more intently. "Ethel?" he cried in astonishment.

Gramma staggered and grabbed the back of a chair. Slowly, she lowered herself into it. "Gaspar," she whispered. "Marie. Bob!"

"What's going on here?" I asked, totally baffled.

"That's what I want to know," said Gramma. Her voice was weak. She sounded terrified.

Gaspar turned to me. "Your grandmother and I were once engaged to be married," he said softly.

"It is you," whispered Gramma. "But how is it possible?"

"It's a long story," said Gaspar.

"He's not kidding," I said.

"Sit," said Gramma. "Tell."

Gaspar sat.

We spent the most of that afternoon at the kitchen table. There were two stories that needed to be told: what had happened to Sarah and me in the last twenty-four hours, and what had happened to Gaspar, Marie, and the other Morleys over fifty years ago.

"We don't know all of it ourselves," said Gaspar, speaking loudly and clearly so that Gramma could hear. "And we won't, unless the Wentar is able to bring back not only my brother, but the clone that had replaced him for all those years. But I can tell you how it started.

"I was, as you know, both a scientist and a magician."

"It was considered a great scandal by those who figured it out," put in Gramma Walker.

"Yes, and an even greater scandal when big

brother here started going out with a woman so much younger than himself," said Marie. "Such is the way of the small town."

It took me a moment to realize she was talking about Gramma.

"Don't fool yourself, Marie," said Gramma sharply. "When I moved to the big city, I learned that people there gossip just as much as small-town folk. More, probably. It's just that you have to be better known to get gossiped about by the 'right' people. Go on, Gaspar. I'm eager to find out why you broke my heart."

"Breaking your heart was the last thing I ever intended," said Gaspar sadly.

"Can we skip the romance and tell the story?" I asked. I was still trying to get used to the idea of Gramma being younger than Gaspar, since she looked thirty or forty years older than him. But then, she had kept on living for the fifty years that Gaspar and his family had been frozen.

Gaspar nodded, his face no longer that of a great lizard, but that of a lean, handsome man. I tried to imagine what it would have been like if things had worked out differently and he had married my grandmother. Grampa Gaspar.

It was too much to wrap my mind around.

"It started when I discovered the secret of

the Starry Doors," he said. "I was angry, because I realized Martin had known it for some time, and had not shared it with me."

"Of course, that was before we found out that Martin was an alien clone, and not our real brother," said Marie.

"True," said Gaspar. "It makes so much of our history different to understand that. Anyway, with Darlene, Marie, Albert, and Bob, I began to explore other worlds. One planet in particular, Zentarazna, held a great fascination for us. In that place, people had learned to shape their own bodies as they wished, to change them as it suited their fancy. Since Marie and Darlene had grown tired of all the attention they got for their great beauty, they quickly embraced the idea of taking on a strange image."

"We tried several," said Marie. "It was fun."

Gramma shot her a glance, and I got the sense that they had not liked each other fifty years ago.

"Of course," said Gaspar, "Albert was always Albert, and Bob's problems started back in Transylvania. They are who they are. It was Darlene, Marie, and I who played at shapeshifting. There was to be a town-wide Halloween party one night—"

"The last time I ever saw you," murmured Gramma.

Gaspar nodded. "The three of us decided to come not in costume, but in our other personas. We thought it would be fun. Alas, that was the night Martin discovered what we had been doing. A great argument broke out . . . and that's the last thing I remember until I found myself standing on the edge of your bathroom sink, looking up at Anthony and Sarah."

Gramma reached out and took his hand. "I cried for a long time after you disappeared," she whispered.

Gaspar put his hand over hers. "I did not expect this," he said. I was startled to see tears in his eyes. Then I realized that even though fifty years had gone by for Gramma, for him it was as if he had last seen her only a day before, seen her young and beautiful, seen her perhaps as the woman he was going to marry.

"And now you need to go to the Land of the Dead," said Gramma, awe and wonder in her voice.

Gaspar nodded.

"Well, I'm going with you," she said.

Gaspar started to protest, but it was pointless. I knew that tone of voice. He had as much of a chance of talking Gramma out of it as I had of sprouting wings and flying—though the way things had been going, that wouldn't have surprised me all that much. Gramma might have been surprised to see Gaspar, might even have felt the stirrings of an old love. But there was no way she was going to miss a chance to visit Grampa.

At eleven o'clock that night, we returned to Morley Manor. There had been some question about whether or not Sarah and I would be allowed to come. Gramma thought it was too dangerous, but when we pointed out what we had already been through, she relented.

A bulldozer was parked in front of the house.

"It was a close call," said Gaspar.

In the house Gaspar led the way down the cellar stairs. We crossed the basement and he opened a door that led to another stairway, one that took us even deeper into the earth.

"There are many ways to the Land of the Dead," he said. "But the deeper you go, the easier it is to get there."

"So the Land of the Dead is underground?" asked Sarah.

"Not really. In fact, from what the Wentar told me, it isn't really anywhere in this world at all. But to go deep in the earth brings you closer to a certain kind of truth. It will help in our journey."

A cobweb brushed across my forehead. The air was cold and damp. I heard Bob whine, and Marie murmur words of comfort.

I counted a hundred and thirteen steps.

"Where did these stairs come from?" asked Marie.

"Martin built them," said Gaspar.

Finally we reached the bottom. The chamber we entered was earthen-walled, but had a solid ceiling, supported by thick wooden beams.

Gaspar instructed us to lie down and join hands. The floor was cool and damp, but he said the closeness to the earth was important. He worked in the darkness, muttering to himself. Every once in a while I heard him strike a match. A weird odor filled the room.

"Close your eyes," he whispered. "Think of those who have gone before."

He said more things, but I am not allowed to repeat them.

I lay in the darkness, thinking of Grampa.

A long time went by.

Suddenly I looked down, and saw a long silver cord. I realized that it stretched back to my own body.

Gramma was floating next to me. Near her, I saw Sarah and Marie. Gaspar was on the other side of me. Even Bob had made it through.

Ahead of us, all around us, was a vast space, filled with a kind of milky mist. Floating through it were the figures of people, some of them sharply defined, others soft around the edges, so it was hard to make them out. Moans and mutters filled the air.

We drifted forward. I heard Gramma gasp.

Ahead of us floated Grampa Walker.

TO BE CONTINUED IN
BRUCE COVILLE'S BOOK OF NIGHTMARES II

Old Mrs. Foss was cranky when she was alive. So Meech should have realized that he shouldn't cross her after she was dead.

LEAVES

Mary K. Whittington

High on a branch of the tallest maple tree, one lone leaf trembled in the autumn wind. Meech willed the yellow scrap to fall, to join the ankle-deep carpet of leaves beneath the trees that crowded old Mrs. Foss's wide front yard. Smiling, he kicked up great rustling swashes of leaves, watched them float groundward. They could stay there forever, for all he cared. Crazy old Mrs. Foss would never make him rake her leaves again. She'd died last month.

Seven autumns he'd worked for her, since he was six and barely able to handle a rake. Mom praised him for being neighborly, but that wasn't the reason he continued to do the job. Mrs. Foss paid him four dollars, more spending money than he ever had at one time.

Still, he dreaded the raking weeks in advance. To begin with, Mrs. Foss always waited until every one of the leaves had fallen, until it took him a whole day to rake them up. Then, she ordered him to come on the one Saturday he'd made plans, like playing football with the guys. Usually, if he could postpone the game until Sunday, he'd wake up to pouring rain.

And no matter what Meech did, Mrs. Foss was never satisfied. From early morning until late afternoon on raking day, she watched him from the corner window of the sprawling gray house, her ugly old housecoat wrapped tightly about her thin shoulders. When she wasn't spying, she yelled at him.

"You, Meacham. Don't forget to rake down by the creek. And you've missed two leaves near the hedge." She punctuated each word with a bony finger jabbed in his direction. "You, boy, don't you know how to use a rake? I should hire someone else, I should."

Meech, trying without success to ignore her, almost agreed. But he thought of his four dollars, gritted his teeth, and kept raking.

When Meech was ten, Dad got hurt at the mill and could not work for several months. Meech told Mrs. Foss he needed more pay, and she promised him a raise. All day, while he raked and hauled leaves, he imagined his mother's face, happy and proud, when he told her he was giving all that money to her, to help out with the groceries. And then Mrs. Foss only paid him one extra dollar. The old witch. Her dead husband had left her plenty of money. Meech had hated her ever since.

From then on, when he finished raking, he almost had to force himself to go to the back of the house and knock on the door. There she met him, wearing her faded green housecoat, torn and unwashed. Meech tried not to focus on the daubs of egg and the brown stains on the front. Her hair, dull and dirty, hung in different lengths as if she'd attempted to cut it herself, and she smelled like mildew. Taking shallow breaths, he watched her dig into her pocket with a shriveled hand, its nails long, yellow, and curved. She extracted a wad of gray tissues, found a limp five-dollar bill among them, and thrust it at him. Without saying thank you, she closed the door in his face, leaving him holding his pay by one damp corner. After he got home, he'd put the bill into the pocket of a pair of dirty jeans going into the next wash.

Strange, Meech thought, kicking leaves before the vacant house, how he could have hated Mrs. Foss so much. She probably hated him, too, maybe because she was jealous of his being young and healthy while she could only move with pain. Sometimes, when he had found himself starting to feel sorry for her, a thought he hid deep within stirred. He should help her, five dollars or no five dollars. But then the hate rose and stilled the traitor thought.

"Meacham." A whisper, like the sound of leaves falling, startled him. He glanced over his shoulder at the corner window. His heart lurched. Behind the glass something moved. He made himself look, and breathed relief when he recognized the reflection of the last leaf floating past the window. And the voice? Imagination, that's what. Nothing was going to scare him.

The maples fenced him in, interbranched above him, their empty twigs twisted against the sky. She'd loved those trees, Mrs. Foss had, probably the only living things she'd ever loved. More than once he had looked out his bedroom window in the morning to see her hobbling among them, touching a trunk here, a branch there, the hem of her housecoat wet with dew. She had cared for them like she would her children, if she'd ever had any, making sure the trees had enough water in the summer, that their leaves got raked every autumn.

Now, he crunched his way between the trees, heading home. At the gap in the hedge he paused and looked back at the lonely gray house, the maples guarding it, and the fir trees behind, separating the property from the community cemetery, where Mrs. Foss lay buried.

Shouldering through the hedge, Meech went in to dinner.

In the middle of the night, the chimes of the grandfather clock downstairs woke Meech from a dream. Someone had been chasing him through leaves, which whirled about him in slow motion. Awake now, he listened for the clock's comforting tick, strained to catch sounds of his father snoring two rooms away, his mother talking in her sleep, the house creaking. He heard nothing. Sitting up in bed, he eased himself over the edge of the mattress to the floor, felt the braided rug beneath his bare feet, rose, and went to the window.

Below was the dark mass of the hedge between Mrs. Foss's yard and his. The moon, nearly full, silvered the gray house, turning the windows into shadowy mouths behind the skeleton trees. From beneath the nearest, a gaunt figure materialized, hardly more than a gray silhouette. Meech shaded his eyes against the moon's glare.

"Mea-cham." A whisper drifted through the partly opened window.

"Who's that?" Meech asked, half to himself.

The figure glided forward, raised a long thin

object above its head. A leaf rake? With a start, Meech recognized Mrs. Foss.

"Mea-cham." She drew his name out in long syllables.

"Go away," Meech said through chattering teeth. "You're dead. I never have to rake your leaves again." He went back to bed to lie stiff and sleepless for the next hour. Just as he was beginning to think he'd had another dream, he heard the whisper again, much closer.

"Mea-cham."

Against his will, he turned his head to the window, to see her floating in the air outside, the moon shining through her face, out her eyes. She pointed the rake at him.

"No." Meech dove beneath the blankets. When he looked again, he saw only the face of the moon. He wiped his sweaty hands on his pajama top, breathed deeply until his heart stopped pounding, and tried to relax. What a night for dreams.

The mysterious silence had given way to normal night sounds—the grandfather clock ticked downstairs, his father snored, the house creaked. Meech stretched, pummeled his pillow into shape, and closed his eyes. But the image of Mrs. Foss stayed in his mind, stealing his sleep. After a long span of twisting and wrestling with the bedclothes, Meech rolled over and listened. Silence.

Slowly, he opened his eyes. The moon no longer shone through the window, but a dim light still filtered across his bookshelves and desk, across the oak-leaf wallpaper. Cold filled the room, a dank cold, heavy with the smell of decay.

"Mea-cham."

The whisper came from the murky corner nearest the door. Meech sat partway up, clutching the sheet under his chin with both hands.

He could not see her, but he knew she was there, lurking in the shadows. He could almost see two gleaming eyes, staring at him. His skin prickled with tiny needles of ice.

He cowered back under the blanket. Whimpering with fear, he curled into a tight ball. When his muscles began to sting with tension, he chanced another quick look. The shadowed corner was empty, but the numbing chill remained in the room, as if she'd left it to remind him of her. After a long while it receded, taking the horrible odor with it.

Sleep was now impossible. For the remaining hours of the night Meech tossed and sweated, reliving the night's encounters. He could think of nothing else. Only when the sky began to lighten did his terror diminish, to change to anger. How dare she try to scare him like that? He'd show her. What's more, he'd get back at her, even if she *was* dead. But how? Meech sat

up, gazed out the window at the dawn, and thought. After a time, he began to smile. There was one way to get even. It would involve raking those leaves, but it would be worth it.

All day, Meech raked leaves and dragged them by the tarpful under the branches of the firs behind the empty house.

"I'll get you, you horrible old witch." He muttered constantly. "I'll get you." His hate and desire for revenge grew with every hour, every trip to the rapidly growing pile.

At dusk, he pulled the last load of leaves to the mound, but left them in the tarp. He rubbed his blistered palms, eased his back, and leaned on the rake. Looking down at it, he saw a crumpled piece of gray-green paper wedged between the tines. A five-dollar bill. He stared, unwilling to touch it, half wondering if the old lady had dropped it before she died, for him to find.

"You're not going to buy me off," he said, finally. "It's not your money I want this time." With his shoe he scraped the bill off and kicked it onto the leaf pile.

As the sun dropped, a wind sighed through the fir trees, and the piled leaves whispered in answer.

"Don't you go flying off," Meech told them

under his breath. "I have far better plans for you."

He pulled the corners of the tarp together, hefted it over his shoulder, and lugged it in between two of the firs. Before him lay the oldest part of the graveyard, many of its tombstones leaning at precarious angles. As soon as darkness fell and he assured himself that all visitors had gone, he skirted the old stones, dragging the tarp beyond the first two rows to Mrs. Foss's grave. He knew where it was, because his mom had made him go to the funeral. He threw the tarp down, unfolded it, and grabbed a huge armload of leaves, crushing them against his chest. He felt their dry tips against his neck and hands, smelled their sweet, dead odor. For a moment he stood still, savoring his vengeance. Then he flung them upon the grave.

"You want more?" he shouted. "You just wait."

Back he went to the pile of leaves, packed more into the tarp, wincing as crisp leaf edges poked into his blisters. The pain fed his anger, gave him the energy he needed to carry the tarp, to hurl even more armloads of maple leaves on the grave. He felt hot all over, his head and back ached, but he marched back and forth until the grave was awash with leaves, until they covered the new, straight-edged stone with its inscription, "Elvira Foss, 1898–1988."

The last load, from the bottom of the heap by the firs, left his hands earth-covered, clammy, and reeking of mold. Stepping back, he wiped them on his jeans.

"There you are, Mrs. Foss. You can rake your own leaves now." He threw the leaf rake into the pile and walked away.

When he had almost reached the firs, he stopped and listened. Something trailed him, whispering between the tombstones. He felt the hair on his arms begin to rise until he realized his follower was nothing but the wind. It gusted between the firs, moaned in the upper branches of the leafless maples. It sang into the service porch when he opened the back door. He thought the wind sang for him, celebrating his triumph.

A stray leaf clung to his sweater. He picked it off, dropped it on the back steps for the wind to play with, and shut the door.

Meech went to bed early, sleeping soundly until the midnight chimes of the grandfather clock woke him. Moonlight streamed in the window, and the awful silence was back. Without wanting to, he stood up and moved to the window. The full moon hung above the tips of the firs, which gyrated in the wind. As he watched, a flock of birds flew up from behind them, across the face of the moon, a flock which broadened until it filled the sky. What kind of birds would flock by night?

They were headed straight for him, and as they drew closer, he recognized them. His stomach shrank to a hard knot, his throat tightened. He forced down a scream.

They weren't birds. They were leaves, flying toward him on the wailing wind. Coming closer and closer. Meech slammed the window shut, but the dark silence ate the sound. He leaped for his bed. Black leaf shapes piled one on another against the window until they blotted out the moonlight, buried his bedroom with smothering darkness. And then, cutting through the stillness, came raspy slitherings against the glass, like a host of spiders trying to get in. The window frame creaked. Just when he thought it wouldn't hold, the sounds ceased, the darkness withdrew.

Meech held his breath. The household drowned in silence. Carefully, he inched back out of bed, and crept to the corner of the window. Nothing clung to the cracks in the frame, and the moon showed him no sign of leaves when he risked raising the window and looking out. If it weren't for the awful quiet, he'd think everything was as usual. He waited, sitting on the edge of his bed, listening hard. Nothing.

But no sooner had he crawled back under his blankets than he heard, on the edge of the silence, the back door click open. He must have forgotten to latch it. He had better get up and do it now, before the wind blew in.

When he had gone halfway down the hall, the rustling began downstairs. He paused at the top step and squinted into the dark below, heard scratching sounds coming nearer, coming up the stairs. Tamping down panic, Meech backed into his room and locked the door. He huddled on his bed, arms wrapped tight around his knees, trying to make himself believe he hadn't seen the masses of crackling leaves swarming toward him.

The wind sighed outside his door and a rattling followed, as if rivers of leaves poured into the hall.

"Mea-cham," came a whisper.

Something scuttled along the bottom of his door.

A leaf slid slowly beneath and stopped, rocking back and forth, its tips curled up like claws.

There are all kinds of unfinished business . . .

GEORGE PINKERTON AND THE BEDTIME GHOST

Lawrence Watt-Evans and Julie Evans

When Uncle Miles called, I happened to be by the phone, so I answered it. "Do you want to talk to Mom?" I asked him.

"Actually, Billy," Uncle Miles said, "I wanted to talk to *you*. That friend of yours, George Pinkerton, the monster expert—does he handle ghosts, too?"

"I don't know," I said. "Why?"

He explained how a friend of his had bought a house and then discovered that it was haunted. Every night about eight the ghost would start wailing and keep it up until after midnight. The friend and his wife and their two kids weren't getting much sleep.

"Do you think Mr. Pinkerton might help?" Uncle Miles asked.

"I'll ask him," I said.

It took a couple of days to talk him into it. Mr. Pinkerton doesn't like to admit that he's anything but a librarian, let alone a world-famous monster expert, but I kept on dropping by the library, talking about how interesting a case it was, and how these folks couldn't sleep in their own house, until finally he gave in. That weekend Mr. Pinkerton and I packed a few things and drove up to Oak Forest to see this ghost for ourselves—or hear it, anyway.

The house was a big old place, more than a hundred years old. The Baxters met us at the front door. A little girl was clinging to Mr. Baxter's leg, and Mrs. Baxter was holding a baby.

They all looked tired. All but the baby had dark circles under their eyes from lack of sleep. Mr. Pinkerton can look scruffy and out of shape sometimes, with his potbelly and his beard that he doesn't trim very often, and the flannel shirts and old jeans he wears whenever he's on a case. But compared to the Baxters, he looked fit as a fiddle.

"Come on in," said Mr. Baxter, and we all went in and sat at the kitchen table. There was another man there. Mr. Baxter introduced him as Jim Kyriakis.

"He's the one who sold us the house without telling us it was haunted," Mr. Baxter said.

"It *wasn't* haunted!" Mr. Kyriakis insisted. "I lived here for forty-six years and never saw a ghost, or heard one, either."

"Well, it's haunted now!" Mr. Baxter shouted. "And it isn't anything *we* did!"

"Okay, tell me about it," Mr. Pinkerton said. "When did the ghost first appear?"

"The day we moved in," Mr. Baxter said, calming down. "I was just getting Jill ready for bed." He indicated his little girl—she was about three years old.

"Did you see the ghost?"

Mr. Baxter shook his head. "No, but we sure *heard* it. It scared the heck out of us. I was trying to read Jill a bedtime story, but every time I said a word, this wailing started. Finally I just gave up, but the wailing kept going, and none of us could get to sleep."

"No story," little Jill added.

"Jill never got her story," Mr. Baxter agreed. "The next night we heard it again. Same time. Same thing happened. I was putting Jill to bed, and just as we were settling her in and starting to read a book, the wailing started." He shuddered.

"Very interesting," Mr. Pinkerton said. "Have you heard or seen anything unusual at any other time of day?"

"No," Mr. Baxter said. "Just at Jill's bedtime."

"Which room was it? Was it always the same room?"

Mr. Baxter shook his head again. "We tried moving Jill to another room after the second night. It didn't help."

Mr. Pinkerton stroked his beard. "Now, *that's* interesting. I read up on ghosts before I came here. Most ghosts are tied to a particular place—usually either the place the person died, or a specific place connected with some unfinished business the person had. That's why most ghosts hang around—because they have unfinished business. Ghosts that do the same thing over and over, as you describe, usually do it in exactly the same place each time."

"Well, not this one. We've tried every bedroom in the house."

"Fascinating!" I could see Mr. Pinkerton's eyes sparkle behind his glasses. Then he turned to Mr. Kyriakis.

"You lived here for forty-six years, and you never heard this ghost?"

"That's right. Not once."

"Did you ever have anyone else stay here? Any family, or friends?"

"Sure," Mr. Kyriakis said. "Lots of times. None of them heard any ghost."

Mr. Pinkerton nodded thoughtfully and looked

at Jill. "Ever have any young children sleep here?"

"Uh . . ." Mr. Kyriakis had to think about that for a while. Finally he said, "I guess not. I never married, you know. Never had any kids of my own. Never knew much about kids, really."

"Sometimes," Mr. Pinkerton said, "it's a place that's haunted. Other times it's a person. Had Jill ever seen or heard any ghosts before you moved here? Or any of the rest of you?" He looked at the Baxters.

They looked at each other. Mrs. Baxter said no, then Mr. Baxter, and finally Jill shook her head.

"Then it's probably the place," Mr. Pinkerton said. "But whatever ghost dwells here never bothered anyone until now." He turned back to Mr. Kyriakis. "Who lived in this house before you?" he asked.

"A family named Turner. I bought the house from old Mrs. Turner when it got to be too much for her to keep up. Mr. Turner was dead by then."

"Did the Turners have any children?"

Mr. Kyriakis shook his head. "If you're looking for someone who can tell you more about the house, you're out of luck. What I heard from their neighbors was that their only daughter died young, of scarlet fever. That was back in the 1920s."

"Could she be the ghost?" I asked.

"She might be," Mr. Pinkerton agreed. "How old was she when she died? Did she die here, in this house?"

"I don't know," Mr. Kyriakis said, surprised. "I never asked where she died. She was only five or six years old, I think."

"About the wailing you heard," Mr. Pinkerton asked Mr. Baxter. "Did it sound like a five-year-old?"

Mr. Baxter looked at Jill. "Could be." He looked back at Mr. Pinkerton. "All right," he said. "Whoever the ghost is, how do we make it stop?"

"I don't know—yet," Mr. Pinkerton said. "I'd suggest that you and your family stay at a motel tonight, Mr. Baxter. Billy and I will stay here and see if we can handle your ghost."

"We will?" I looked up at Mr. Pinkerton. "Oh, sure! We will."

So that night there were just the two of us in the house, me and Mr. Pinkerton. We got a pizza delivered for supper, and then we sat around talking and reading for a while—he'd brought a box of books about ghosts. About a quarter to eight Mr. Pinkerton clapped his book shut and said, "I think it's time to begin our vigil." Together we crept up the stairs to Jill's room at the back of the house and settled in to wait for the ghost.

We sat there, doing nothing except getting bored waiting for the ghost to show up. We weren't talking, for fear of scaring it off. Finally, at about five past eight, I said, "Nothing's happening."

"No," Mr. Pinkerton agreed. "Obviously, something is missing—just as it was when Mr. Kyriakis lived here."

"Do you think it's Jill?" I asked. "Maybe she's doing it. One of the books I was reading downstairs said that some hauntings are caused by kids with psychic powers, usually girls, and not by ghosts at all."

"That's one theory about poltergeists, yes. I don't think it's the case here. As for why nothing has happened, the wailing always started when Jill was being put to bed; maybe that triggers it. Jim Kyriakis never had any kids to put to bed."

"Well, neither do we," I said.

"I can put *you* to bed," Mr. Pinkerton said.

"Huh?" I said. I protested that I wasn't a baby and it wasn't my bedtime and I could darn well put myself to bed.

Mr. Pinkerton waited until I was done and then said, "Do you want to hear this wailing ghost? Then pretend I'm putting you to bed."

"Why do you have to put anyone to bed?

Why don't you use a doll?" I pointed out one of Jill's.

Mr. Pinkerton looked at the doll and shrugged. "I think you'd be more convincing," he said.

I couldn't really argue with that. I grumbled a little more, but I knew he was right, and I did want to hear the ghost. I brushed my teeth, then said, "I didn't bring any pajamas." I'd figured on sleeping in my clothes. I hadn't planned on being "put to bed."

"Can you fake it?" Mr. Pinkerton asked.

"I guess," I said. I took my shirt off, then turned it around and put it on backward to pretend it was pajamas. Then I got into Jill's bed.

"Good night, Mr. Pinkerton," I said. "But you can forget about a good-night kiss."

He laughed. "Don't worry. I don't think we have to go that far." But he did pull the blanket up to tuck me in. I felt really stupid.

Then we waited again.

Nothing happened.

After a few minutes Mr. Pinkerton looked around the room thoughtfully. He spotted the bookcase.

"Ah! Mr. Baxter said he was reading Jill a bedtime story the first time." He crossed the room and got a book from the shelf—a Dr. Seuss book, *Green Eggs and Ham.* He opened it.

That was when I first thought I heard something, or maybe just *felt* something, as if some-

one—or something—was sucking in its breath in excitement.

Mr. Pinkerton started reading, and before he was halfway through the first "Sam I am," the wailing started.

It was deafening. It *did* sound like a little kid, only louder than any little kid I ever heard in my life. That ghost was just yelling its lungs out. I clapped my hands over my ears.

I couldn't make out any words for sure. It was mostly just wailing. I thought I'd be scared when I first heard a real ghost, but it was so loud I couldn't think clearly enough to be scared—I just wanted it to *stop.*

Mr. Pinkerton tried to say something, but I couldn't hear him over the ghost. He tried again, then got up, beckoned to me, and led the way downstairs.

The wailing followed us—and I could almost hear something bumping down the stairs, as well. When I turned to look, I even thought I saw something, but then it was gone.

Mr. Pinkerton led the way out onto the porch; the wailing ghost stopped at the front door, and by the time we were halfway down the driveway, we could talk and be heard again.

"She's haunting that house," Mr. Pinkerton said. "No particular room, but definitely the house, and not a person."

I nodded. "It sure sounds like a little kid to

me," I said. "I bet it *is* the Turner girl. But why is she here?" Then a thought struck me. "Hey, didn't you say ghosts usually have some unfinished business to take care of?"

"So the books say."

"What sort of business could a five-year-old have?"

"That's a very good question," Mr. Pinkerton said, stroking his beard. "And why would the bedtime reading set her off?"

"Maybe she doesn't like to hear people reading," I suggested.

"Have you ever met a little kid who didn't like to be read to?"

I had to admit I hadn't. "Maybe she didn't like that particular book," I said.

"And maybe there's a connection between your question and mine," Mr. Pinkerton said. "Did your parents read to you at bedtime?"

"Huh?" I asked. "Well, they stopped when I was eight or nine—I was reading my own books by then."

"But before that they read to you?"

"Of course!"

He nodded thoughtfully. "And did they always read you an entire story at each sitting?"

"No, sometimes they'd read me a chapter each night until we finished a whole book. Man, sometimes I'd even want to go to bed early just so I could find out how the story came out. . . ."

I stopped.

"Unfinished business," I said. "She wants to hear the rest of a book."

"The one her parents had been reading when she died. And it's not *Green Eggs and Ham.* That one wasn't written yet."

"Besides, that's a one-sitting book."

"I didn't bring any storybooks," Mr. Pinkerton said. "Let's see if the library is open."

The library was nearby and stayed open until nine one night a week. We were lucky—this was the late night. We hopped into Mr. Pinkerton's car and got there with twenty minutes to spare. (I fixed my shirt before we went in so I wouldn't look like a geek.)

Mr. Pinkerton headed straight for the children's room. Since he's a librarian himself, he was able to practically zip past whole shelves—he knew a lot about which stories were written too recently and which were really old. When the children's librarian asked us to please take our books to the desk because they were closing, he had a big stack.

"It probably isn't any of these," he said as we walked back to the car. "It could be something I never heard of. But, on the other hand, if a book is good enough that that poor little girl has been waiting seventy years to hear the ending, it may still be in print." He hefted the books. "Most of these are classics, certainly."

When we got back to the house, the ghost was still shrieking and wailing. I thought I heard her yell, "You promised!"

"She throws quite a tantrum," Mr. Pinkerton said as we walked up the steps to the porch.

We winced when Mr. Pinkerton opened the door; that ghost was *loud.* She seemed to be on the stairs. We marched on, back up the stairs, and she followed us.

In Jill's room Mr. Pinkerton opened the first book to chapter two and started reading—there wasn't any point in trying chapter one, because if she hadn't already heard it, she wouldn't care about the book.

She just kept yelling when he started chapter two of *The Wind in the Willows,* and after a couple of paragraphs he gave up and tried the next.

Peter and Wendy wasn't any better, nor the next book, nor the next. I picked the books and handed them to Mr. Pinkerton; I gave him the books I thought a little girl from the 1920s would have liked.

We kept going until after midnight. We'd worked through almost the entire stack by then. My ears were ringing from all the yelling, and I was beginning to think I'd go deaf. But then Mr. Pinkerton started reading chapter two of *The Wizard of Oz.*

I didn't expect much—I mean, nothing else had worked, and besides, I'd seen the movie, and it had regular sound, and I thought the ghost must be from the silent-movie era. But the book must've been a lot older, because the wailing trailed away, and after a moment a little girl's voice spoke from thin air and said, "Did that part."

Mr. Pinkerton and I looked up, but we couldn't find where the voice was coming from. Finally we looked at each other. Mr. Pinkerton grinned and flipped ahead to chapter three.

"Did that, too," the voice said.

When Mr. Pinkerton got to chapter eleven, "The Wonderful Emerald City of Oz," he read a few paragraphs, expecting the ghost to speak up, but she didn't. He looked at me; I didn't say anything. He continued reading.

When he finished chapter eleven, he looked up again and started to close the book.

The ghost let out a shriek. "More!"

Mr. Pinkerton started reading chapter twelve.

The Wizard of Oz has twenty-four chapters—we weren't even halfway! Mr. Pinkerton read on, until his voice gave out. Then I took a turn.

I was afraid the ghost wouldn't like it, since I don't read anywhere near as well as Mr. Pinkerton, but she didn't seem to mind. She didn't say anything, as long as we kept reading.

It's a pretty neat story. It's really different from the movie, with more stuff happening. I liked reading it aloud, except I got sleepy and my voice started to go. So Mr. Pinkerton took over again for the last couple of chapters. It was almost dawn, and I was half-asleep, when he finally said, " '. . . And oh, Aunt Em! I'm so glad to be at home again!' " and clapped the book shut.

We listened for the ghost's reaction, and it came—very faint, but very real. Mr. Pinkerton and I smiled at each other and tiptoed out of the room. It was much too late to drive all the way home, so I went to sleep in the guest room. Mr. Pinkerton had forgotten to ask which bedroom he should use, so he slept on the couch downstairs.

When we woke up, he called the Baxters at their motel, and they came back home, relieved and grateful—though not entirely sure whether to believe us at first.

But the ghost was gone. The last thing anyone heard from her was the sleepy, contented sigh she made when Mr. Pinkerton and I finished reading to her that very late night.

In the dark, in the night, strange things lie waiting. Sometimes they need our help. The trick is knowing when . . .

A CRY IN THE NIGHT

Nancy Varian Berberick and Greg LaBarbera

Peter woke with a start. He stared at the ceiling, his mind still blurry with the last shred of nightmare.

Ghostly moonlight shimmered through the window. A brittle tapping broke the silence. Tap-tap. Tap-tap. Like fingers rapping the windowpane.

Curious, he slipped out of bed and crept toward the sound. He hugged himself as he wound through stacks of unpacked boxes. His feet grew colder with every step on the wood floor.

Tap-tap.

Peter drew the blue curtains aside. Shadows of crooked tree limbs spread out like dark cracks on the ground. Wind howled, blowing snow across the frozen yard.

Peter brought his face within an inch of the window. His breath fogged the pane. He wiped it away . . . just as a dark, bony hand swooped down at him.

He jumped back, tripping over a box.

Then, a sheepish smile on his face, he realized it was only a wind-whipped branch from the old oak by his window. Feeling foolish, Peter went back to bed.

Outside, the wind moaned, rising and dropping. On the edge of sleep he thought he heard a voice: "Help me! Help me, please!"

But that was only the wind crying.

A shudder rippled down Peter's back. He pulled the blankets tight to his chin.

Surely that's all it was. Wind.

Peter sat at the breakfast table, munching a piece of toast. His father scanned the paper, while his mother pulled dishes out of boxes. They'd moved into this big old house in Miller's Creek only two days ago, but his mom was determined to have everything in order as quickly as possible. He thought of all the boxes piled around the house and groaned inwardly. There would be a lot of work to do today.

A gust of wind flung sparkling snow against the kitchen window. Peter glanced into the yard, then back to his breakfast. This wind wasn't like last night's, he told himself. This wind had no voice.

Trying to sound casual, he said, "Did you guys hear anything last night?"

His father looked over the edge of the paper. "Sure did, and it kept me awake most of the night."

Peter leaned forward.

"I thought I'd never get to sleep with your mother's snoring."

Peter's mother looked over her shoulder. "Now, James, you know everyone's supposed to think it's *you* snoring."

His father winked, but Peter didn't smile.

"I'm serious, Dad. Did you hear anything last night?"

"Nothing—except the wind. Why?"

Peter took a gulp of orange juice, considering whether to tell his parents about the voice he thought he'd heard. Now, in daylight, the whole idea of a mysterious voice was starting to seem foolish. "Never mind," he said. "Dad's probably right. It must have been the wind."

His father lowered his voice to a deep whisper. "Are you sure? Maybe we have a ghost lurking around."

Peter stared at the woods running darkly behind the house. A chill touched the back of his neck.

But he shook it off. "Yeah, right, Dad. A ghost."

* * *

Wind moaned around the eaves. In the fireplace, flames snapped and popped, casting flickering shadows on the wall, like dark fingers reaching. The screams of zombies, the shrieks of their victims, filled the living room.

Peter sat huddled in a blanket, a bowl of popcorn on his lap. *Night of the Living Dead* was his favorite video.

"I don't know what you see in those awful movies," his mother had said as she and his father got ready to go out for the evening. "But have a good time anyway. We'll be back before midnight." She'd kissed him and tousled his hair. "Remember: There are no such things as zombies and ghosts."

Peter never knew how to explain what he liked about horror movies. He simply knew that the thrill of fear was somehow, well . . . enjoyable. Like the screaming excitement of a roller-coaster ride. No fun when you think about it, and great fun when you're doing it.

After the survivors dragged the stunned zombies into a giant pile for burning, the light from the TV faded. The room grew still. In the hearth, the fire had fallen to glaring embers, like glowing, evil eyes.

Outside, the wind sobbed.

"Help me! Please, help me!"

Peter sat still as stone. That was no wind. That was a voice, and he couldn't pretend it wasn't.

"Help, please!"

Slowly, he stood and walked to the back door. His hand shook as he wiped steam from the pane.

"Help me! Oh . . . please . . ."

The voice sounded as if it belonged to a kid his age. It seemed to be coming from nearby. And it sounded frightened.

"Who are you?" Peter called, his own voice quivering. He stood frozen in the silence, as if made of the same ice that hung from the roof.

"Hello?" he tried again. "*Where* are you?"

Peter gasped as footprints appeared in the snow, running from the house, toward the woods.

The voice whimpered, "Peter, you've got to help me."

That did it. Whoever it was, the ghost had spoken his name.

He grabbed his jacket and a flashlight. It was cold outside, and dark. But that didn't matter.

He had to find out what was going on.

Wind whipped his hair. Peter's breath came in small tufts of steam. He clicked on thc flashlight and squatted next to the footprints. They were about the same size as his own tracks and led right into the woods.

"Peter, help! I'm scared!"

So am I, Peter thought. But he followed the

snowy prints and the beam of his flashlight into the woods.

Trees closed around him. The woods were far darker than he'd imagined. His stomach tightened. Wind blew, cold on his neck. He pulled up his jacket collar and followed the footprints, ready to go as far as they'd take him. Someone was in trouble. Someone needed his help.

After what felt like a very long time, the tracks ended suddenly in a small clearing, leaving Peter facing a steep hillside. Snow-dusted boulders jutted from the bank. Jumbles of brown, withered vines snaked around them, writhing to the ground. In the moonlight and shadow the rocks and vines seemed to take on the shape of a huge, hairy face, twisted with malice.

"Help me, Peter. I'm scared!"

The voice came from behind the rocks—from *inside* the hill. A chill rolled up Peter's spine. This ghost hunt didn't seem like such a good idea anymore.

"Peter! I'm in here. Help me!"

A pale hand reached out of the hillside, right through stone, beckoning.

Peter's eyes grew wide. He let his breath go in a ragged scream.

He spun around and stumbled out of the clearing. He ran hard, following his own footprints back toward the edge of the woods. The flashlight's beam leaped wildly across the trees.

"Peter! Help!"

The voice followed him, wailing. Wind blew right at him, like cold hands trying to push him back. Trying to keep him from getting home! Peter tripped over a snow-covered root and scrambled back up again, running, running.

At last he reached the house. He bolted the door and ran into every room, clicking on all the lights. Then he went back to the kitchen and kept his gaze riveted to the back door. All the while that he waited for his parents to return, he grasped the flashlight tightly in his hand. As if it were a club.

He heard nothing of the voice until the next night.

Peter stood in the attic, among the boxes of old books and summer clothes. He looked around, waiting for his father to bring up the next box. The last family had left a few things behind, some old crates and a stack of newspapers piled near a window. Dust drifted through a shaft of sunlight as Peter sifted through the papers.

One of the headlines snagged his attention.

SEARCH ABANDONED FOR JACOB DANIEL. BODY NEVER RECOVERED.

Peter drew in a sharp breath—and coughed on the dust. The paper was dated ten years earlier. Below the headline was a picture of a boy about Peter's age.

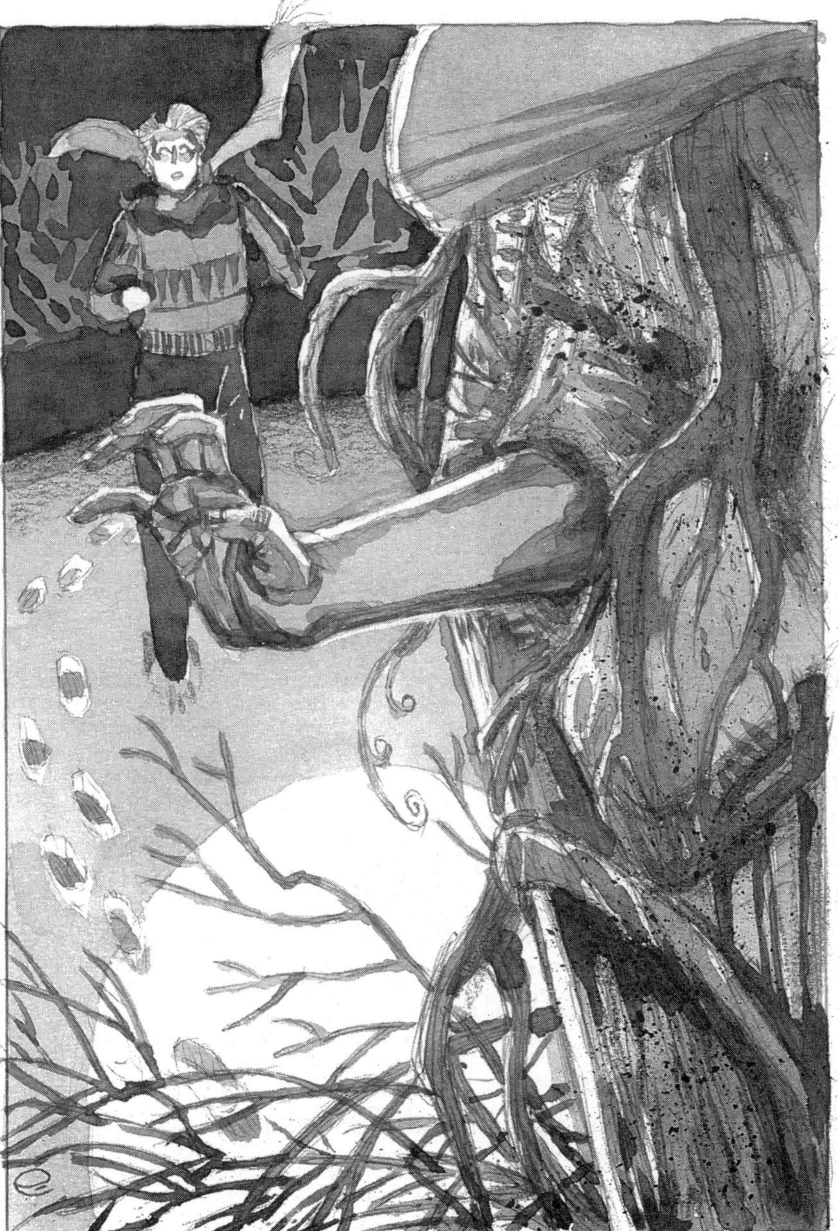

"State and local police have given up the search for eleven-year-old Jacob Daniel of Miller's Creek . . ."

Jacob Daniel!

Miller's Creek!

The voice, the ghost—it must be Jacob Daniel.

Peter closed his eyes, trying to think. Everyone knew ghosts roam only because they have unfinished business among the living. Jacob Daniel was surely haunting because his body had never been found.

And all this while he'd been haunting unheard. Ignored. *Remember,* Peter's mother had said, *there is no such thing as a ghost. . . .*

But there is! Peter knew it, if no one else did.

Suddenly the air in the attic felt close and thick. Poor Jacob. He wanted someone to find him, somewhere inside the hill. No wonder he sounded so frightened.

Peter's father heaved a large box up into the attic. "That's the last one, champ."

Peter thought quickly as he pushed the box over to the others. "Okay, Dad. I'm going to explore the woods out back for a while."

And save a ghost, he thought.

"No way. You still have all the boxes in your room to unpack. You can explore tomorrow."

Peter bit back his frustration. It never did any good to argue with his father. "You got it, Dad."

But Jacob Daniel could have been a kid just

like him. Now he was lost and scared and alone. Peter wasn't going to let him stay that way. He'd unpack his room, just as his father said he had to.

Then, tonight, when Jacob's ghost called again, Peter would go searching for a body.

Peter's stomach rolled and surged, just as it always did at the start of a really scary movie. But this was no movie; this was his real life, and he was about to go into the haunted darkness to find the place where a boy had died. He slipped into his jacket.

"Peter!" the ghost called, breaking the silence of Peter's room. "Peter! Help!"

Peter took a breath to steady his courage. He slid his window open and stepped out into the night. His sneakers crunched on crusty, frozen snow.

Flashlight in hand, Peter slipped into the woods. The moon stayed hidden among the clouds. He looked up and blinked as big, fluffy snowflakes dabbed his cheeks.

Jacob's ghost had left new footprints, but soon they wouldn't be easy to find.

Peter hesitated. His heart pounded in his ears when he thought about what might have happened to Jacob. Had he gotten lost? A cold little ripple of fear scooted along Peter's neck. Or had the poor kid been murdered?

Peter shivered, from more than cold. He

looked back at the house, dark and silent. He couldn't go back and tell his parents what he knew. They wouldn't believe him. He squared his shoulders and kept walking. He would have to do this himself.

When he reached the clearing, Peter stopped at the foot of the hill.

"Peter, help me," the frightened voice cried through the night. "I'm in here!"

Once more the ghostly hand emerged through the rocks and vines. Maybe it was a trick of the faint light, but the hand didn't seem pale and white this time. Instead, it glowed faintly blue, like shadows on snow. The hand beckoned, then sank back into the hill.

Peter pounded back the urge to run. Jacob Daniel was in trouble, trapped and doomed to haunt as a ghost till his body was found. That glowing hand had to be Jacob's, showing him the way to the body.

"I have to do this," Peter said aloud. In the darkness his own voice sounded small and alone. "I have to help him."

Moving a bunch of vines aside, Peter uncovered a small crevice. He aimed the flashlight's beam into the fissure. A small passage snaked farther into the hill.

From inside, Jacob's ghost cried, "In here, Peter! Help!"

"Okay," Peter whispered to himself. "Just go

in and come right back out. Once I find him, he can rest in peace."

He took a deep breath and squeezed into the opening. He could feel the jagged edges of rocks even through his heavy jacket as he wiggled his way into the crevice. When he finally passed through, the cave opened enough for him to walk. Steeling himself, he went deeper under the hill. He hadn't gone far when the beam of his flashlight fell upon a brown skeleton.

Peter inched his foot toward the tangle of bones. They looked so small and lonely. He tapped them with his sneaker.

They creaked and rattled.

Sadness mixed with satisfaction. Peter whispered, "There, I've found you, Jacob. Now you don't have to haunt anymore. I'll get someone up here in the morning to give you a proper burial."

He waited for an answer. None came. The voice seemed to have vanished.

Curious, he said, "What did happen to you, Jacob? Did you fall and hit your head or something?" He turned the smooth skull over with his toe. No crack there to tell of an injury. And all the rest of the bones looked whole. "Why didn't you just crawl out of here?"

Silence filled the cave, like a pressing weight.

Then a stone rattled, somewhere to his left.

Peter turned sharply. Fear shot through him. The flashlight's beam bounded all over the rocky walls. He steadied his hand—and saw another skeleton.

Then a deep, hollow voice—not Jacob's!—echoed in the cave. "Because once I get you children in here, there is no way out."

Dull rumbling shook the ground.

Peter's gut went cold. The flashlight fell from his hand. The crazily rolling beam made shadows leap up from the rocky floor, like darkness clawing at his feet.

He spun around and came face-to-face with a terrifying wraith. Stringy strands of hair wormed around a blue and ghastly face set deep with dark creases. The ghost reached for Peter with outstretched arms, from which phantom flesh peeled in rags and shreds.

Peter bolted for the entrance, only to find his way out blocked by a boulder.

He threw himself against the rock, pounding with his fists.

It didn't budge.

In the light flung up from the floor, the wraith seemed three times as tall as it was. It shuffled toward him, laughing.

"What are you?" Peter cried.

"Someone who feeds on fear and drinks up terror. I've been under this hill forever, and I don't wake up often. But when I do, I know how to get what I need." The phantom's voice changed suddenly to Jacob's. "Oh, help me, Peter! Help me!"

Deep, echoing laughter taunted Peter.

"Jacob Daniel was never found," said the wraith. It pointed toward the second skeleton. The light from the fallen flashlight made the shadow of its clawlike hand huge. "Neither was she, and neither were the others. One by one they came to me. I doubt they'll find you either, Peter Myers. Your tracks in the snow will be covered by morning."

Peter turned, heart racing, to look right, then left. All he saw was cold stone with no way out.

No way out!

The cave walls seemed to be closing in on him. He beat his fists against the stone until his knuckles bled. He screamed until his voice was no more than a ragged rasp.

Finally he slid to the ground, his back against the boulder.

The phantom snatched up the flashlight and swung it round and round its head. Shadows spun. Light leaped. And the ghost flung the flashlight against the wall, shattering it.

Darkness fell like blindness. Fear, which used to touch Peter like a delicious thrill, grasped him now and squeezed the breath from his lungs. He couldn't breathe. He couldn't move.

He heard the ghost shuffling toward him.

"No!" Peter wailed.

But, of course, no one could hear.

April stared as her twin sister, Janice, rushed into the room and slammed the door. In her hand was a photocopy. She dropped it onto the bed and said, "Look at this, April! It's a copy of a newspaper article I found at the library."

April rolled her eyes. They had all of winter break to finish their homework assignments on the history of Miller's Creek. Leave it to Janice to get started on the first day of vacation.

Then she glanced at the photocopy and saw the picture of a boy who couldn't have been much older than they were. The article was dated fourteen years earlier.

SEARCH ABANDONED FOR MILLER'S CREEK BOY. BODY NEVER RECOVERED. . . . *The missing boy, thirteen-year-old Peter Myers of Miller's Creek* . . .

April gasped, a little afraid, a little delighted. "Janice, this kid used to live right here in Miller's Creek!"

Janice nodded. "I told you that was a ghost we heard last night."

"Do you think it's Peter Myers?"

Janice's eyes glinted eagerly. "I'm sure of it. And I think he wants us to find him."

One of the things I always hope to do with these anthologies is see how "far out" we can get and still have the stories fit the main topic. For those who know Mel Gilden's writing, it should be no surprise that he has come up with the weirdest ghost in this collection. Weird is Mel's specialty. I like that in a writer.

HAUNTED BY A PIG

Mel Gilden

While I was sorting through an ancient wooden cigar box, throwing away the shortest pencil stubs and the erasers that over many years had turned into smooth, useless rocks, the little hairs on the back of my neck began to tickle, as if they were marching around like ants. I turned slowly to see my paperback novels rising into the air like a fountain and falling back to the floor. Comics flapped through the air, circling the fountain of novels like boldly colored birds.

"Mom!" I called. Maybe for once she would arrive in time to see the evidence for herself.

Of course, by the time Mom walked up the stairs and along the hall to my doorway, the show was over. "What?" she asked.

"Don't you notice anything different about my room?"

"It looks worse than it did before," she said as she glanced around. "Did you put anything at all in that lawn-and-leaf bag?"

"Not much," I admitted.

"The next time you call me in here, it better be because the place is on fire, or because it's clean. Understand?" She continued looking around the room with disapproval. "Your uncle Max will be here tomorrow, and his welcome-home party is the day after."

"I know, Mom. A hundred people," I said. I had never met my mother's brother, Max. All I knew was that he somehow made a living traveling around the world, and that once in a while he sent me weird gifts: masks made from tree bark, little clothespin people, a coconut-shell door knocker—real *National Geographic* stuff. Most of the gifts were still somewhere in my room. I knew I hadn't thrown them away.

Keeping stuff, even stuff I didn't really need, had always been kind of a problem. It was as if the stuff owned me instead of me owning it. The mess was so embarrassing, I didn't even invite friends over. Depressing, huh?

Not even my parents were clear on exactly

why Uncle Max traveled so much. "He's in business," my father would say. Mom thought he was a journalist, mostly because his articles on ancient pottery, rare books, and home electronics—to name a few topics—occasionally appeared in a magazine called *Real-Sounding Countries.* I thought everything he did was a cover for his real occupation—I was sure he was a spy.

"Your aunt Lucille will be here."

"I know, Mom," I said. Dad's sister, Lucille, was not actually a bad person, but she liked to have things her own way. Mom was worried that she would peek into my room, see the battle zone, and accuse her of not raising me properly.

Aunt Lucille lived at the other end of the country, so she did not visit often. But when she did, she always made Mom a little tense. And when that happened, Mom made *me* a little tense. Of course, I was a little tense already. I didn't exactly enjoy living with all this junk—especially now, with Uncle Max and the big party coming. I was determined that either I or the mess would triumph once and for all.

"Why not just nail some boards across my door?" I suggested eagerly. "We'll trap the pig in here, and I can move into the den."

I suspected the thing haunting my room was a pig. What else could be so determined to keep my room looking like a sty? I had no idea how it had gotten there, though without it my room probably would have been pretty messy anyway. The pig just made the situation worse.

"Oh, Howard," Mom said. "Your father's talked to you about that imaginary pig."

"It isn't a regular pig," I said, aware of how lame I sounded. "It's invisible or something. But you can hear it."

We both listened. In a corner a stack of old *TV Guides* with science-fiction covers fell against a plastic bag full of plastic bags. "See," I cried, pointing. "It's back there in the corner."

"That's no pig," Mom assured me. "Your stuff is piled so high, I'm surprised more of it doesn't fall over. Clean up your room." Mom smiled and ruffled my hair and went back to the kitchen.

While I collected my comics into a stack again, I wondered if my life would have been easier if I'd kept the pig a secret and just admitted my own natural messiness.

Either way, Uncle Max would arrive within hours, and my room was still haunted by a pig.

I felt even worse because the rest of the house was such a white-glove test—everything in its place, no dust anywhere. No wonder the pig stayed in my room. The neatness outside probably frightened it. I wasn't frightened by neatness, but it seemed just as crazy in its way as my mess. I felt as if I were living in a museum.

My parents and I stood in the living room. Mom had decreed that we mustn't sit on any of the furniture because it would leave a depression in the plastic covers. I was too excited to sit anyway.

The doorbell rang and I ran for it. I threw open the front door and gaped. The man standing there was worth a gape or two. He was tall and had shoulder-length hair so purple he might have washed it in grape juice. The jumpsuit he wore was fire-engine red with bright green and yellow splotches on it. Everything about him was big—his eyes, his nose, his hands. He wasn't particularly handsome, but the lines and creases in his big face made him seem as friendly and comforting as an ugly old dog.

"Uncle Max?" I asked, never doubting that's who it was.

"You must be Harvard," the man said, and handed me his suitcase. It was surprisingly heavy, as if it were full of bricks.

"Howard," I said while I struggled with the suitcase.

"Whatever. I am delighted to see you." He reached out and shook my free hand, engulfing it in his enormous paw.

Uncle Max hugged Mom and shook hands with Dad, and everybody said how nice it was to see everybody else again. I showed him to the guest room, which was just down the hall from my room. He would have to pass my room to get anywhere.

"Hungry?" he asked. He took the suitcase from me as if it were filled with soap bubbles.

"Howard," I said, correcting him automatically.

"Howard, are you hungry?"

"Yes, sir," I said, feeling silly about my mistake.

"Me too," Uncle Max said. "Come on, we'll talk to your parents."

Max and I walked along the upstairs hallway, and I relaxed when he passed the closed door of my room. Mom hadn't let me *nail* it shut, but at least it was shut. He stopped at the top of the stairway and sniffed with his nose high in the air. "What's in here?"

"Nothing. Just my room." I died a little, knowing Mom would never forgive me for embarrassing her like this.

"May I?" Max said. Without waiting for my answer, he thrust the door open as if hoping to catch someone stealing cookies or changing their report card or something. It was dark inside, and he switched on the light.

"What a barn," I suggested before Uncle Max had a chance.

"Absolutely," Max said. He sniffed the air. "You are haunted by a pig, are you not?"

"Huh?" I exclaimed, surprised by his question. I couldn't smell anything.

Uncle Max did a Sherlock Holmes number, walking around the room, sniffing the air, peering into my plastic lawn-and-leaf bag, picking up stuff and putting it down exactly where he got it.

"You mean it really is a pig?" I finally asked. "I'm not crazy?"

"The spoor is unmistakable," he said, laying a finger aside his nose.

"Spoor?"

"The track or trail of a wild animal—in this case of the phantom pig. It is said that many of them live down in La Cabana. I myself have come across evidence of the creature—his spoor—but never the creature himself."

"You have?"

"Come along, young Harold," Uncle Max said. He gathered me inside one huge arm as he doused the lights and closed the door. "We will eat the eat," he said as he peered at me. "And then," he went on, "we will talk the talk."

"And then will we pig the pig?" I asked.

"Eat the eat," he said. "Talk the talk."

When Uncle Max suggested we eat at a La Cabanan restaurant, Dad recoiled as if Max had released a bad smell.

"It'll be fun," Mom said, smiling with difficulty. She was not much into experimental cooking. Her idea of exotic food was spaghetti sauce you made from powder that came in a little silver packet. If I wanted adventure I went to one of the local fast food joints.

"Come along, then," Uncle Max said, using much the same tone on my parents that he'd used on me.

Max's car turned out to be a Ketalbi Manticore, and it was totally wonderful. It was painted in the same way as his jumpsuit, and the wheels were thick and enormous. I couldn't decide whether the thing looked more like a Jeep or a tank. He explained that it was on loan from the La Cabanan consulate. I sat in front with Max while Mom and Dad sat together in the back.

The La Cabanan place was called the Screaming Lizard. The menu was all in La Cabanan, so Uncle Max had to order for everybody. The lizard Uncle Max ordered tasted like chicken, if chicken came from Mars. Mom and Dad just smiled uncomfortably and pushed their food around, but I enjoyed the whole experience.

"So, Max," Dad said, "do you spend a lot of time in La Cabana?"

"Oh, yes," Max said. "A lot, these days. You'll notice I am wearing my traditional La Cabanan camouflage outfit."

Mom looked at him with astonishment. "A red suit with green and yellow splotches is camouflage?" she asked as if she didn't believe him.

"*Yama yama*," Max said, "which in La Cabanan means 'for sure.' You may have noticed that my hair is purple, just like the famed La Cabanan flower, the feygehleh. More camouflage."

"La Cabana must be a really strange place," I remarked.

"About average for that part of the world," Uncle Max assured us.

By the time we got home, I wanted to scream. We had eaten the eat. Now it was time to talk the talk. And, if I was lucky, to pig the pig.

"We'd like to hear all about your travels," Mom said as we entered the living room.

"As well you should," Uncle Max said. "I've led a strange life. But right now I have something of vital importance to discuss with Herman here."

"Howard," my dad said.

"Whatever," I said, grinning like a fool. It didn't matter what Uncle Max called me as long as he got rid of the pig. Before the parents could protest, Uncle Max hustled me out of the living room and up the stairs.

While I switched on the light, Uncle Max sat down on my bed. He closed his eyes and folded his hands before him. "Uncle Max?" I said as I closed the door behind me.

Uncle Max opened his eyes and studied me, his eyes wide and a little crazy looking. "Tell me about the pig," he said.

I would rather have had Uncle Max tell *me* about how ghost pigs came to live in La Cabana—the story was probably interesting. But I didn't want to distract him from the business at hand. "I wasn't even *absolutely* sure it was a pig till you told me," I said.

Uncle Max nodded.

"The pig won't let me clean up," I explained. "My room gets worse all the time. The junk is taking over my life. I don't even know how the pig got here."

"Spirit pigs are indeed rare outside La Cabana. Of course, they're rare *inside* La Cabana, too. Have you received anything from there lately?"

"Not lately," I explained. "The only thing I ever remember getting from La Cabana was that box of bananas you sent when I was in first grade."

Uncle Max went pale. "Then I am afraid," he said with difficulty, "that I am responsible for your problem."

"Huh?"

"It is said that in some ways La Cabanan spirit pigs are like tarantulas. They can travel hidden in loads of bananas. I must not have known that when I sent . . ."

I stared at him in shock. "You mean," I said, "that my room is a mess because once upon a time you sent me a gift box of fruit?"

Uncle Max nodded, crushed. He looked so whipped that I couldn't stay angry at him. Besides, how the sucker had gotten in was less important than how to get rid of it before the big party. With Uncle Max there to help, I had a real chance to clean up my room at last. "So, what are we going to do about it?" I asked, hoping to take his mind off his guilt.

"Huh?" he asked, still preoccupied. He shrugged. "We don't need to get rid of it, I suppose. When your room is clean, it will just go away—back to La Cabana, perhaps."

"But we can't clean up till the pig is gone," I explained. "It won't let us. I've tried. Believe me."

"Nonsense," Uncle Max said. He picked up a rubber band and shot it into the open mouth of my lawn-and-leaf bag.

The rubber band shot back out and struck Uncle Max sharply on the leg. He reached down to rub the spot. "I am sorry to see this is an extreme case."

"Maybe instead of cleaning up the room, we should get rid of the pig first."

"And take it where?"

"Back to La Cabana?"

Uncle Max frowned. "I was hoping," he said, "you would suggest somewhere closer to your home."

"I'll think of something," I assured him.

"Very well," he said as he stood. "We must begin immediately! Your room has been a mess long enough!" He upended a shopping bag full of trash, dumping dead flowers of tissue, candy wrappers, attempts at folding a paper fortune-teller, first drafts of school essays, flash from plastic-model kits, and pencil sharpenings onto the floor.

"What are you doing?" I cried.

Max walked to the stack of comic books and began to throw them all around the room as if he were dealing cards. "We must make your room so sloppy that the pig will show itself."

"What good will that do?" I asked, though the idea of actually *seeing* the pig at last was pretty exciting.

"La Cabanan folklore is not clear on that point," he said as he studied the room through steepled fingers. "We'll need more clutter."

"Right," I said, and hurried downstairs to the kitchen, where I found Mom and Dad sitting at the table eating baloney sandwiches and drinking coffee.

"Where are you going with that?" Dad asked as I picked up the garbage bag. Coffee grounds were heaped over banana skins. The bag smelled awful, and there was a wet spot near the bottom. The pig would love it. "Uh, Uncle Max wanted it," I said.

Mom and Dad got up and followed me back to my room, making me feel guilty even though I hadn't done anything wrong and I was under adult supervision and everything.

Immediately my parents banged on the door. "Max?" they called. "Howard? What's going on in there?"

"Spread this around," Max said, pointing to the garbage bag. "I'll take care of them." He slipped out the door.

"Here you go, pig," I said. "Have a good time." I didn't want to actually touch the stuff—this was slimy food garbage, not dry paper trash—so I just kind of shook out the contents of the bag. My room had never smelled before—except to Uncle Max—but it now gave off a pungent odor of rotten fruit salad.

I heard an oink! I was sure of it! I had never heard an oink in my room before! Maybe Uncle Max had the right idea, after all!

Max came back into the room, rubbing his hands together. "Is that a pig I hear?" he asked.

"*Yama yama,*" I said. "What did you tell my parents?"

"I told them the garbage was for a project in archaeology. I told them we were going to study it and see what we could learn about your family. I told them it would be educational."

"They bought that?" I asked with amazement.

"I can be *very* convincing."

The evidence forced me to agree with him. An hour later I heard my parents pass by on their way to bed, but they didn't knock on the door again that evening.

"There it is!" I cried, pointing. "I can see right through it as if it were a ghost."

"It is a ghost, Humphrey. I told you that."

Ghost or not, it did, in fact, look exactly like a small pink pig. It was dancing on its hind legs atop a small mountain of beef bones, orange peelings, and some lumps of yellow chicken fat.

"I had always heard," Uncle Max said, "that the La Cabanan spirit pig was a fun-loving creature. Now we mix well and hope for full materialization."

We picked up handfuls of action figures and flung them into the air. We mixed books with comics, and video-game cartridges with model kits. We threw around crumpled arithmetic assignments and grapefruit rinds. The room looked as if wild gorillas had fought a battle there, but with every move we made, the pig became a little more energetic, a little more solid. Soon it was all there.

Uncle Max and I stood in the corner watch-

TV

ing the pig sit in the middle of the floor scratching vigorously behind one ear with a hind foot.

"What do we do now?" I asked.

"Now we capture it and haul it away," Uncle Max said.

"Can we do that? I mean, can we even touch a ghost?"

Uncle Max thought about that for a moment. "I believe so. After all, the floor of your bedroom supports it. And if it is solid enough to touch your possessions, it must be solid enough to capture." He pointed to the left. "You go that way. We will use a classic pincer movement."

I had no idea what a classic pincer movement was, but when I moved to the left, Uncle Max moved to the right. Slowly, carefully, we approached the pig.

"Now!" Uncle Max cried.

We jumped at the pig, and at the same moment it leaped away. We chased it around the room, slipping and sliding through the muck, leaping at it and catching only armfuls of trash.

At last Max and I collapsed in opposite corners of the room, and we glowered at the pig as it twirled and jigged—as energetic as ever.

"It has undone me, Heathcliff," Uncle Max said, and groaned as he massaged one shoulder. "I *am* sorry."

The situation looked bleak, all right. The

state of my room had gone way beyond wild gorillas at their worst. Mom would have a fit, and then Aunt Lucille would have a fit, and I would probably have to go with Uncle Max when he returned to La Cabana.

"I was wondering," I said after a few minutes, "if what keeps the pig here is not me or the room, but the clutter *in* the room."

"It's a theory," Uncle Max agreed. "But so what?"

"Let's take the clutter somewhere else," I suggested.

"Have you decided where, exactly?"

"To the dump."

"A good choice. But you should know better than I that the pig will not allow us to take the clutter to the dump or anywhere else. After all, isn't taking the clutter somewhere else pretty much the same thing as cleaning up?"

I thought over Uncle Max's argument. It was solid, but I saw a way out. "You said the La Cabanan spirit pig is a fun-loving creature. Maybe if we put on a good enough show, the pig won't notice what we're actually doing."

He stared at me, his eyes widening. "It's worth a try. And if we succeed, you will go down in La Cabanan folklore." He snapped his fingers. "Quickly, now," he said as he stood up. "We will need many lawn-and-leaf bags."

The pig didn't notice any of this. It was nosing through an old wood-burning set I hadn't looked at in years.

"No problem," I said. With a new enthusiasm I ran to the kitchen for the box of bags.

When I got back, Uncle Max and I laughed as we scooped up armful after armful of stuff and dumped it into the bags. Uncle Max began to sing a strange wailing song—some kind of La Cabanan work song, I supposed, because we picked up its heavy rhythm. We worked in a cleaning frenzy such as my room had never seen.

Casually we gyrated into the hallway. Among the bulging lawn-and-leaf bags piled there we found the pig also dancing to the La Cabanan melody. I picked up a couple of heavy bags in each hand, as did Uncle Max, and we strutted in time down the stairs and out to his Ketalbi Manticore. The pig followed us, oinking in time to Max's song as it leaped around us in circles.

Because the street was dark and quiet, I could hear Uncle Max, though he only whispered his song. He opened up the back of the Manticore, and I could see there was plenty of room, enough for a couple of lions, maybe. We threw our bags into the back of the Manticore, and the pig climbed aboard. We hurried to the front and got in.

"Please navigate," Uncle Max said as he started the engine.

Driving through the empty streets to the other side of town took us more than half an hour, but the pig seemed content to lie among the lumpy lawn-and-leaf bags. Though once when I checked the back, he looked directly at me. His eyes were large, liquid, and a little sad. I could have sworn he knew what we were up to.

When we arrived at the dump, I jumped down to unhook the chain across the entrance. Uncle Max drove in as far as he could, right to the edge of the main heap.

Uncle Max started his song again as he opened the back of the truck and tossed me the first of the bags. I flung it as far as I could up the heap. And the second one. And the third. And so on until the back of the Manticore was empty except for the pig, who looked around, bewildered.

Uncle Max spoke to the pig in La Cabanan and patted his thigh as if trying to attract the attention of a dog. The pig glanced at him, looked away, then leaped out of the Manticore. When it saw the mountains of trash, it ran off and was soon lost among them.

We both stood there trying to ignore the smell while we enjoyed the coolness of the night. Somewhere out of sight the ghost pig was digging around enthusiastically as it oinked the La Cabanan folk song.

"Sorry to see the spirit pig go, Hiram?"

"Yeah. It was kind of a pet. But now that it's gone, maybe I can get myself in gear and clean up." I smiled. "It'll be kind of a new experience to be able to find stuff."

"Yama yama," Uncle Max said. He slammed the back of his Ketalbi Manticore, and we walked back to the front seat.

I was tired, but when we got home and I looked at all the leftover junk still in my room, I had to finish the cleanup. Uncle Max pitched in and helped. We didn't dust or vacuum, but when we were done sorting, stacking, and putting away, the room looked as if a normal kid lived there. It no longer looked like a pig sty.

The next day Uncle Max's welcome-home party was a big success. The high point came when Max and I taught the relatives the La Cabanan folk song we'd sung to the pig the night before. We even leaped onto the couch and danced a few steps to it, and nobody seemed to mind.

"You've done a wonderful job with that boy," Aunt Lucille said, making my mother smile.

"Yama yama," I said.

In a book of ghost stories, you really ought to let at least one ghost speak for itself. Meet Jonathan. Has he got a story for you.

CALL ME GHOST

by Lael Littke

Call me Ghost.

I had another name during the fourteen years I was alive, but I've forgotten it. That's what more than two hundred years of going nowhere will do to you.

I can't give an exact count of the years I've been in this old house. After the first century, you start to lose track of time. I have hardly any memories of when I was alive except big things, like in 1783 when the news came that our American colonists had won the war against the British. Even a ghost wouldn't forget a major event like that, especially with this house so close to Boston where it all started.

I don't remember when or how I stopped

being a living boy and became a ghost. I don't know what I have to do to get finished with it.

I wish I did know. I mean, there must be *something* after death besides just hanging around. I'd like to get on with it.

One more thing sticks in my mind from the time before I died, and that's the word "patience."

So I've tried to be patient. Two hundred years of patience. Try it sometime. It gets so that there isn't a whole lot that's fun any more. Not changes in the house, nor new electronic equipment, nor even new owners, though I do update my vocabulary every time someone moves in.

The present owner of the house is forty-something with a short, no-upkeep hairdo and a neat but no-frills clothes attitude. Milda Cartwright. I like her. She writes mystery stories for kids. She saw me her first day here. She just shrugged and said, "They warned me that I might see you, Ghost, but if you won't bother me, I won't bother you."

Then, one day when I was sunning my ectoplasm in the southeast bedroom upstairs I heard Milda yell "Patience!" It seemed to come from the front door.

Why was Milda shouting the one word I remembered from my past?

Sunlight energizes me, so putting myself into

a high-gear float, I hurried down the stairs. It isn't easy because you have to overcome all the air currents that can blow you right up to the attic or down to the cellar if you're feeling weak. That's why ghosts usually hang out in those places, you know.

There was a girl standing in the doorway when I got there. She was not much younger than I'd been when I died.

Suddenly I remembered something. Patience wasn't a quality, as I'd thought for so long. A scrap of memory told me Patience was a girl's name. A girl I'd known a long time ago.

The girl in the doorway wore cut-off black shorts, a black T-shirt, black socks, and black lug-sole shoes. She carried a black duffel bag.

"Come in, Patience," Milda said. "I'm so glad you could visit."

Another Patience! Was this a coincidence or what?

It was easy to see that Patience wasn't as glad as Milda was. Gloomily she allowed herself to be hugged. Then she saw me. I was almost totally materialized because of the sunlight. I expected her to scream or something, but all she did was look at Milda and say, "I see you've been to the Rent-a-Ghost store."

Milda laughed. "He came with the house. Don't you love him?"

"Yeah. Right." Patience glanced my way. "Just stay out of my space, Ghost," she snarled.

Words came back to me. "Take yourself out of my territory."

They'd been said in another time by another Patience.

I wished I could say something in answer to the rude command this Patience had thrown at me. Sometimes I can do a bit of hollow hooting, but I'd used too much energy at that moment by materializing.

So I turned and let the air currents carry me where they would, which turned out to be the attic. That was better than the cellar. For some reason I hated the cellar.

I peeked down the attic stairs long enough to see Patience get settled in the sunny southeast bedroom, along with a collection of *National Geographic* magazines and a cello.

I stayed out of her space for several days. But I heard her and Milda talking, sometimes far into the night, and Patience sounded as cranky as a tail-twisted cat. She didn't want to be there. She didn't want to be anywhere.

Patience hated thc world.

Nobody came to be friends with her, which isn't surprising considering this old house is way out in the boonies. I don't know how far since I haven't been outside since before the

Revolutionary War. There are certain barriers that keep me in.

Patience spent most of her time alone in her sunny room.

The other Patience, the one in the tatters of my memory, had stayed to herself a lot, too, although there'd been a time when she'd said, "Jonathan. . . ."

JONATHAN! That was my name. Jonathan.

"Jonathan," Patience had said, "would you like to play a game?"

What game? Why was I remembering this?

The present-day Patience didn't speak to me at all. She just sawed away every day at her cello. I heard its moans and groans from the attic. Lonely sounds, they were.

One day, after sitting in a shaft of sunlight, I drifted down and started harmonizing with the cello. "Hooooo," I went. "Hooooo."

The cello stopped its mournful mooing. With a deep sigh, Patience turned to look at me.

"I can do better than that hollering into a tin bucket."

That ticked me. I wanted to tell her I'd sung with better musicians than she was during the years I'd occupied that house. They'd usually gotten spooked (pardon the pun) when I tried it, but at least they didn't throw insults at me.

"You'd better stick to haunting," she said.

"Hooooo," I said.

"Yooooo," Patience said. "That's hooooo."

To my surprise, she giggled. It was the first happy sound I'd heard her make since she came. It didn't last long, but at least I knew she wasn't *all* gloom.

She stared at me.

I waited.

"Can you speak, Ghost?" she asked finally.

"Nooooo." Raising some ectoplasm to point toward Milda's writing room, I managed to say, "Compoooooter."

"Computer!" Patience squinted at me. "How did you learn about computers?"

"Smooooots," I said, knowing that wouldn't mean a thing to her.

The Smoots had lived in the house before Milda bought it. There were three really cool kids who liked to play with me. They had a computer, and after watching them I got inside to look around and found I could operate it. Don't ask me how because I can't explain. I could make words on the monitor while still seeing and hearing what the kids were doing and saying. It took a lot of energy, but if I could soak up enough sunlight during the day I could communicate.

Patience leaned her cello against the bed. "Come on, Ghost," she said. "We're gonna check this out."

Marching into the room where Milda sat

clicking away on the computer, she said, "Did you know Ghost has been messing with your computer?"

"NOOOOO," I protested.

I mean, I hadn't been *messing* with it. Just using it when Milda left it turned on while she ate lunch or walked around thinking through a plot. I've been writing my official ghostography, of which this will be a part. I keep it in a file that can be opened only with a code word so Milda won't be bothered by it.

Milda clicked off a couple more sentences before she turned to look at Patience and me.

"It's okay, Ghost," she said. "I don't know why I didn't think of asking if you could communicate."

I knew why. Milda forgets about everything when she gets going on a story. She forgets me and dinner and the Fourth of July. But that's okay. I like her stories. They're some of the few bright spots in my miserable existence.

Milda stood up, waving a hand at the computer. "Feel like saying something now, Ghost?" She turned to Patience. "This is wonderful, honey. Now we can talk with him."

"I'm thrilled," Patience said.

I knew how much.

My energy was fading. The only words I could make appear on the screen were *Need sunlight*.

"Oh, my dear," Milda said. "I didn't know that. Patience will be happy to share her sunny room during the day."

Patience wasn't *happy* to share, but she did. I didn't like it any more than she did because of the way she tortured that cello.

But I got my sunlight every morning which gave me the energy to begin communicating with Milda. And Patience, too. She said she couldn't care less, but she showed up every time I floated to the computer.

Of course the first thing Milda wanted to know was why I was there and how long I'd been there.

I made a ? appear on the screen since I didn't know.

"Ghosts have to hang around until they've made up for something terrible they've done," Patience said.

"Ghost didn't do anything terrible," Milda said. "He's too gentle."

"Well then," Patience said, "something terrible happened *to* him. He has to hang around until somebody figures out what it was before he can go on."

I wasn't surprised that she knew a lot. Any girl who collects *National Geographic* magazines must read a lot of stuff.

That other Patience read a lot, too. We didn't

have many books except for the Bible and a few others, but she read them over and over again.

"Maybe," Patience said, "if we could get him to tell about himself, you could sell it as a story, Aunt Milda."

I worked the computer so that the words *I could be ghost writer* appeared on the screen.

Patience looked surprised, and for the second time I heard her giggle. "Hey, Ghost," she said, "that's a real hoooooot!"

That's when we became friends.

For the next couple of weeks life was pleasant, if you could call my condition life. Patience began wearing clothes that weren't all black, and she gave that mournful cello a rest.

Milda told us we could use her computer when she wasn't working, so whenever I'd soaked up enough sunlight Patience and I played computer games. Sometimes we just talked. I mean she talked and I worked things inside the computer.

Patience was surprised to find out we were the same age.

She told me her parents were separated and it seemed like the end of the world. "What's the matter with them?" she demanded. "They promised to do the 'till death do us part' thing when they got married, so how come Dad moved out?"

She said they'd sent her to live with her

Aunt Milda for a while because she'd been so obnoxious from being so angry at them. "I've decided I'm not going home until they get back together," she said. "That's my top wish."

I told her how my primo wish was go on to the next stage of existence, if there was one.

"Poor Ghost," she said. "Don't you know anything about your life?"

Not really, I put on the monitor. *Except that my name is Jonathan.*

"I'd rather call you Ghost," Patience said.

Letters came for her from both of her parents. She tossed them aside, unread, until I said I wished *I* could get a letter from home. I wished I even knew if I'd *had* a family.

That day she opened all her letters.

She cried when she read the latest from her mom. "They're getting a divorce," she said. "Guess I'll be here as long as you will, Ghost, because I won't have a family either."

She rubbed at her eyes with a shredded tissue, then went on. "You must have had a family, Ghost. Some kind of a family. Do you think they lived here?"

I shrugged, which took less energy than operating the computer.

She thought for a while. "We'll find out."

The first thing she did was ask Milda about the background of the house.

"Didn't you read the letter I sent you and

your parents when I moved here?" Milda said. "This house used to belong to our family."

Patience ducked her head. "Mom showed the letter to me, but I didn't read it. I wasn't exactly communicating at the time."

"Never know what you might pick up by tuning in." Milda swung around on her chair so that she was facing us. "I don't know a lot except that our ancestors lived here before the Revolutionary War."

"Wow." Patience looked at me. "Maybe we're related, Ghost."

For some reason I doubted it. The Patience in the fragments of my memory didn't seem like a relative.

I started working the computer. *Is Patience a family name?* I asked.

Patience shrugged. "How should I know?"

Milda gazed at her for a moment, then abruptly turned back to the computer. "I've told you all I can," she said. "How about you going to the library and doing some research, Patience?"

I had the impression that Milda knew more than she was saying. But it did seem like a good idea to get Patience interested in doing something.

The next morning she headed unenthusiastically for the library.

"Waste of time," she stated when she came home. "All I learned was what we already know—that our family lived here. The librarian said I should check the Historical Society."

"Go tomorrow," Milda said.

"Yuck," Patience said.

She came home happier from the Historical Society. "Hi, Jonathan Prescott," she greeted me, smiling.

Another memory slammed into place. I floated swiftly to Milda's computer. She moved back to make room for me. *My name!* I said on the monitor. *Jonathan PRESCOTT!*

"You lived next door, in a house that's gone now," Patience said triumphantly.

"Goooood wooooork," I hooted. But I needed to know something else. On the computer I asked, *Did you find anybody named Patience*?

"No," Patience said. "But I'll keep looking."

The next day she could hardly wait to go to the Historical Society. When she came home, she said, "That place is full of neat stuff. And guess what? A Patience did live here. Patience Cartwright. My great-great-great-something grandmother!"

It sounds unghostly, but I'd swear a shiver slid down my spine. Was this what I'd been waiting for? A descendant of Patience to release me from my eternity in this old house?

"I'll tell you something else," Patience said. Excitement sparkled in her eyes. This was a different girl from the one who'd shown up on the doorstep dressed all in black. "Listen to this, Ghost. The lady at the Society helped me find some old diaries. One belonged to Patience's mother. She was a midwife and kept a record of a lot of stuff, most of it pretty dull. But she said you and Patience were betrothed, whatever that means."

Betrothed! Yes! Another memory surfaced.

For a change I could give Patience a bit of information. *Means engaged*, I wrote.

Patience nodded. "But you were so young."

Yes, I said, remembering. *Our parents arranged it. We were to be married when we were sixteen. At first Patience wasn't all that happy about it.*

"She must have got to like you later," Patience went on, "because her mother said she daydreamed about you. But she said you disappeared one day when you and your parents were here visiting. Some people thought you didn't like Patience and ran away."

I wouldn't have done that! I loved Patience, even before she loved me.

But I'd been only fourteen. *Maybe I did run away*, I typed.

I didn't think that was it, though. Why would I be doomed to haunt this house if I'd run away?

That other Patience—did she marry somebody else? I wrote.

"Oh, sure," Patience said. "Otherwise I wouldn't be here, Ghost!"

Then she quickly added, "But the diary said she grieved for you for a long, long time."

So she'd cared. It made me happy to know.

"If I can just find out what happened to you," Patience said, "maybe we can send you on your way." She gave me a little smile. "But I'll miss you when you go, Ghost."

Maybe you'll go home soon, too, I wrote.

She shook her head. "Not if my parents don't get back together."

Patience went to the Historical Society the next day and I sunned myself in her room. I wanted to have lots of energy.

She was excited again when she returned. "I found another old diary," she reported. "Written by a guy named Philip who lived here before the Cartwrights. He told about building secret rooms in the house to hide people who were rebelling against the British."

"There's that tiny one behind the fireplace," Milda said. "Not so secret anymore since everybody knows about it."

"I know," Patience said. "But there was another one. In the diary Philip said he was digging a room in the cellar."

I was thinking about the one behind the fireplace. The Smoot kids had loved it. Now, suddenly, it brought back more memories. I remembered Patience saying, "Jonathan, would you like to play a game? Would you like to hide and I will seek you?"

My family had been visiting her family that day. She and I were bored with the older folks' conversation, so we'd played the game. Patience hid first, and I'd finally found her in that little room behind the fireplace, but only because she'd giggled.

Then it was my turn to hide. And I'd gone . . . where? *Down* is the only word that came to mind. Down where? To the cellar? The cellar that I hated?

The cellar where the old diary said a new secret room had been started?

I hurried to Milda's computer. "Mooooove ooooover," I hooted, wishing I could say please. But it's not a hootable word.

On the computer I wrote out what I remembered about the game Patience and I had played. *Maybe we should go look for another secret room,* I wrote.

"In the cellar," Patience said. Her eyes grew large.

I remembered the Smoot kids knocking on the panelled walls of the old cellar. They'd wanted to believe there were secret passageways down there, but they'd never discovered any sliding panels or anything else. So hadn't Philip finished his second secret room?

Milda and Patience went down the cellar stairs. I drifted fearfully behind them. Milda thumped on each panel, but they all sounded the same.

But they didn't all *feel* the same to me. One spot felt cold and it was as if I were suffocating, which isn't a feeling you get very often when you've been dead for a couple of centuries.

More memories came. I'd been in the cellar on that day of the game. There'd been no panelling then, just the rough dirt walls of a root cellar. A stack of old, dusty apple barrels had filled one corner.

I'd moved them aside, intending to hide behind them.

I'd found a narrow tunnel back there. The entry was supported by slim lengths of wood.

Sliding partway into the cold, earthen tunnel, I'd carefully pulled the barrels back to their original places so no one could tell they'd been moved. Then I'd crawled further in.

It was a perfect place to hide. Patience would never find me there, I remembered thinking.

She didn't.

The unfinished tunnel was only about four feet long, and as I crawled around I knocked out the flimsy supports. The entry collapsed.

I was trapped. Without light. Without food or water.

Without air.

That's where my memories ran out.

"Loooook," I told Milda and Patience. I raised some ectoplasm to point at the section of panel where I felt cold.

They got the message. Finding a crowbar, Milda broke through the panelling. Patience found a garden trowel and began to dig.

She cried when she saw the gleam of bones in the small space behind the collapsed tunnel entry. She came over and put her arms round me, something the other Patience had never had a chance to do. They closed on nothing, of course, but I could feel her warmth.

"I love you, Ghost," she said.

Three days later, my bones had been removed and buried in the old cemetery where tombstones totter with age. I thought that might release me, but I was still there in the house.

When Milda and Patience came home from the graveyard, we talked for a while by way of the computer.

The Cartwrights probably never even knew about the tunnel, I wrote.

"They didn't have a clue," Patience said. "That's why they thought you'd run away." She started sniffling again.

Suddenly she grinned. "Hey, Ghost, if you'd

lived and married that other Patience, you'd be my great-great-great-something grandfather."

She was silent for a moment, then she said in a thoughtful voice, "But things don't always work out the way they're supposed to."

I figured she was thinking about her parents who were supposed to love each other for as long as they lived—but didn't.

"Maybe you just have to go on anyway," she added.

Milda smiled. "Interesting, isn't it, Patience, how much you can learn about life from a ghost?"

It was then I realized I'd done as much for Patience as she'd done for me.

As I have that thought, I begin changing.

Hurriedly I form words on the computer. *Something is pulling at me.*

That's the way it feels. Like something drawing me away somewhere. Gently, but persistently. It scares me a little. Am I about to find out what comes after death?

I'm trying to hang back, but the pulling is irresistible.

Patience is leaning close to the screen. "Do you think you're going on, Ghost? To wherever ghosts go? What's it like?"

Misty. Like a foggy winter day. I can barely make the words appear.

"Go for it, Jonathan," she says. She's quiet for a moment. "Maybe I'll go home, too."

After that Patience starts calling me, her voice soft and blurry through the mists. *"Jonathan! Jonathan!"*

Or is it the other Patience?

"Patience," I call back. "I'm right here."

Suddenly she is beside me, the soft homespun of her dress brushing against me. "I've found you," she rejoices. "It's been such a long time, my dear Jonathan."

"Patience," I say, and I know our long-ago game of hide-and-seek is finally over.

The mists are clearing. I see now where we are going. Together, Patience and I. . . .

* * *

(NOTE: The above story was found in its entirety on Milda Cartwright's computer when her niece Patience, after many hours of searching for the right code word for the file, tried "CallMeGhost." To our knowledge, this is the first official ghostography ever published.)

Many songs have a haunting quality, and music can stay with us long after those who have made it are gone.

AFTER YOU'VE GONE

Michael Markiewicz

The interscholastic talent show was only two days away, and as Richard struggled to find yet another note on his guitar, his teacher, Mr. Smentz, was shaking his head sadly. Richard had just practiced this piece with him in the studio. He had gotten through it without a single mistake, but now, sitting in the principal's office, it was a different story.

Mr. Delfones, the principal of Bridgeport Elementary, looked down at the sixth-grader in dismay. He and his secretary both winced at the missed notes and obvious mistakes.

"You're sure he's your best student?" said Mr. Delfones sourly, as Richard scratched another string on the old Epiphone.

A month earlier Richard had agreed to be one

of the students to represent the school. Mr. Smentz had told him how his playing could help Bridgeport win its first talent competition—and a five-hundred-dollar grant for the school. Richard had agreed to do it, mostly for Mr. Smentz, but now he was regretting his decision.

"You're playing in the key of A. So it's an E," Mr. Smentz whispered, pointing to the first string.

Richard's fingers ached from making so many F chords, but it wasn't the pain that was bothering him. He squared himself up, went back to the beginning of the last measure, and started again.

F major, E, hold, D, G sharp, A, E, hold, D, rest, C, D, E.

"Well," said Mr. Smentz weakly, "I'm sure he'll get the hang of it before the show."

"But, John," insisted Mr. Delfones, "we *need* that grant. Maybe we should use the Gomez boy instead?"

Mr. Smentz waved Richard off silently and took the principal across the room, behind the big desk. Quietly, but not quietly enough for Richard to miss, he assured Mr. Delfones of his student's ability.

"In the studio he can play like you wouldn't believe. He's the best student I've ever had.

Professional quality. His fingers are like magic. He just has a little stage fright."

"You think you can cure him of it—by Saturday?"

Mr. Smentz looked back at Richard, who pretended he hadn't heard anything.

The gray-haired instructor rubbed his chin thoughtfully. "I know of something that just might do the trick."

"Like what?" the principal said.

Mr. Smentz didn't answer. He just smiled and walked back toward Richard. "I still think you should represent Bridgeport in the competition," he said gently. "What do you think?"

Richard wasn't sure.

Ever since his grandfather had died the year before, Richard had simply lost his nerve. When he played for Mr. Smentz or his mom, he sounded like a genius, but Gramps' death had taken something from him. His mom and Gramps were the only family he'd ever known, and now that Gramps was gone, Richard found it hard to believe in anything—including himself.

In fact, it was only because of Mr. Smentz's prodding that Richard had continued his lessons. His teacher had done a lot to fill the hole in his heart, and he appreciated the old man's faith in him. Still, it wasn't enough to muster the courage to play for a real audience.

"Richard," began his instructor as the principal approached them, "I know you can do this. How many hours did you play 'After You've Gone' this week?"

"Um, at least an hour a day."

"I don't think you played that an hour every day!" broke in Mr. Delfones.

Richard looked down at the carpet and glanced into the corners of the office. He *had* practiced it every day, faithfully.

Mr. Delfones shook his head again.

"Just give him a chance," Mr. Smentz pleaded.

"Okay," the principal said gruffly. "Just do your best. For the school."

"I'm sure I'll do better if I practice it some more," Richard answered. "I'll do two hours a day."

But both he and his teacher knew it wasn't simply a matter of practice.

Mr. Smentz took Richard back to the studio in the rear of the auditorium and wrote out the next week's assignment.

"Richard, I want to talk to you about something," he said as he scribbled the exercises. "Where do you practice?"

"In my room. Why?"

The old man sighed. He seemed to be deciding something important.

"Perhaps," he offered, "you should try practicing somewhere else."

"Somewhere else? Like where?"

"Do you know the old building on Rantoul Street by the train station?"

"You mean the one with all the windows boarded up and the writing on the walls?"

"That's the one. Did you know that was once a jazz club?"

Richard shook his head.

Mr. Smentz smiled. "That was *some* place back in the forties. All the best players came there."

Richard wasn't impressed. He was thinking about how he was going to let Mr. Smentz down. The man had become almost like a grandfather to him, and he just knew he was going to blow it at the show, no matter how much or where he practiced.

"If you could go back in time to those days . . . Lightning Hopkins, Wes Montgomery, even Django," continued his teacher. "Oh, you should have heard the jam sessions there."

Richard couldn't contain his lack of enthusiasm.

"So?" he said weakly.

Mr. Smentz smiled.

"Here's the key," he answered, pulling a long metal thing from his guitar case. "The acoustics are out of this world."

Richard looked at the huge key suspiciously. It wasn't like any key he had ever seen. It was thick, and the part that went into the door was shaped in a strange figure, almost like a G clef.

"It's all right," said Mr. Smentz. "I own the place. I got it from my old teacher."

"You want me to play in an old abandoned building?" asked Richard suspiciously.

"I keep it up. There's electricity and the water is turned on. It's safe; even the smoke detectors work."

"So why don't you open a nightclub?"

Mr. Smentz smiled again. "I play there once in a while . . . when I feel like I'm losing my touch, or when I just can't seem to get a song to work. But it's a private place, and I guess I'd like to keep it that way."

"You think it'll help if I play in an empty club?" Richard wondered aloud.

"It might. I've sent a couple of other students there over the years, and they seemed to learn something. Play up on the stage. Maybe it will get comfortable after a while."

Richard certainly hoped so. He put the key in his pocket and packed up his guitar and music.

"Should I go there tomorrow?" he asked with a sigh.

Mr. Smentz nodded and made another odd grin.

* * *

The lock clacked loudly as Richard turned the immense key and pulled open the old club door. Inside, it was dark, and as he put his school bag down, he could see a haze of dust that hung thickly in the air like fog. In the center of the room was a single table with three chairs. Near the edge of the light from the street was a wide set of stairs that led to a humble, empty stage.

He moved his bag inside and found a light switch near the bar. A single light came on. He went back and shut the ancient door, then glanced around cautiously. He couldn't believe he was doing this.

He had told his mother he was going to practice after school, so she wouldn't worry. But he didn't tell her he was doing it in some old, broken-down building by the train station. Even though Mr. Smentz had sent him there, she probably would have thought it was a dumb idea. And, at the moment, so did he.

At first he felt weird when he put one of the chairs on the stage. Then he got out his music stand and began to play. He looked around the room again and wondered if this would really help. He concentrated on the tune and slowly began to lose himself in the music.

He played the way he knew he could. His fingers struck the arpeggios with a real sense of style—not at all as he played when someone outside the studio was watching.

But as the old Epiphone came to life in Richard's hands, so did the room around him. He was near the middle of the song when it started. By the time he had reached the second page, there was definitely something going on. But it was only when he came to the first repeat that Richard really noticed.

There were people in the room!

It wasn't just a few who might have come in through the door to see who was playing in the abandoned building. The club was suddenly smoky and glowing, and the hum of more than a hundred strangers surrounded Richard as he gaped in utter shock.

"I must be going nuts," he whispered as his left hand stopped on the C major.

Everyone was looking at him—everyone—and just who *were* they?

Then he heard a rustling behind him just offstage and saw a thin, dark-skinned man standing in the shadows.

"Go ahead, go," insisted the stranger, pointing to Richard's guitar.

But Richard was terrified. Had he time-traveled? Was he hallucinating? What was going on?

He was about to run for his life when he saw the images begin to fade and then blink out like boats floating down the river and out to sea at night. Their light slowly dimmed and then disappeared. All but the thin man in the back.

"Well, they're all gone now!" spat the man as he wandered onto the stage.

Richard wasn't thinking about the strange crowd. He was worrying about how to get out of the place in one piece.

The man smiled and pulled a chair from behind the curtains. He was in a direct line to the door. Richard was shaking so bad, he knew he could never outmaneuver the wiry-looking figure.

"It's okay, kid," said the stranger. "I'm just a ghost, is all. Like all them."

Richard felt his hands tremble.

"I'm not going to hurt you, okay?"

"O . . . o . . . kay," said the boy.

"My name's Skinny. What's yours?"

"R—ri . . ."

"That's some dumb name, Ririh. Your mama call you that?"

"It's Richard," gasped the boy.

"Oh, Richard! That's cool. Man, you got some licks for a kid, Rich!" said Skinny, nodding to the boy's guitar.

"My licks?" asked Richard, who was still looking for a way out.

"Your chops, man. Your playing. You're good."

He didn't know what to say.

"But you can only keep the crowd here if you play. See, this place comes alive when there's music in it. Music's got magic, you know. But you stopped playing. It don't mean a thing if it ain't got that swing, man!"

Richard shook slightly.

"They really appreciate a good jam, but . . ."

Skinny paused and studied his guest carefully. Then he sighed and made a sad frown.

"Well," said the ghost, "I can see you want to run out of here, so I won't stand in your way. But could you tell me one thing before you take off screaming like some crazy kid?"

"Su—sure," stuttered Richard.

"What's your problem?"

"My problem? I don't have any problem."

Skinny laughed a low, knowing laugh.

"You wouldn't be here if you didn't, man. John doesn't give that key to just anybody."

Richard felt the large metal key in his pocket and began to wonder. "John?" he asked.

"John Smentz."

"You know Mr. Smentz?"

"He's been taking care of this place for a long time. Ever since I showed him how to put some soul in his blues."

"You were his teacher?"

"No, I just gave him a few pointers here and

there. But you were sent because of a problem of your own. Now, what is it?"

Richard looked hard at the ghost. He didn't seem that frightening, really. In fact, he seemed kind of nice.

"Um," Richard started, "my teacher told me to practice on this stage."

Skinny stared at him. "Why?"

"He said I should get used to playing on a stage so I can do it in front of people better."

The ghost paused for a moment.

"You got stage fright?"

Richard nodded and explained, "I'm supposed to represent my school in a talent show tomorrow. I'm going to bomb."

He was so upset by that thought that he completely forgot whom he was talking to. He looked down, hating himself for being such a coward.

Skinny got up and walked to the stairs. He reached underneath, putting his ghostly arm right through the boards in the steps, and retrieved a transparent guitar. Without missing a beat he slammed his chair next to Richard's and placed the instrument on his knee.

"Let's see how good you are. Go!"

Richard couldn't believe this was happening. But he did as the ghost ordered.

His hands moved to their positions as Skinny tapped out the timing and called,

"One, two—one, two, three, four."

The music started slowly, and it took Richard nearly six measures to get into it. But as he heard Skinny's backup, his fingers started to move instinctively. The old ghost's sweet chords and lively action were like sparks to Richard's imagination. Skinny's style was so smooth and inviting. Richard's hands flew across the fret board, and when they came to the second repeat, he did something he had never tried. He improvised.

In a magic moment his fingers became like an extension of his thoughts, and they plucked out strains like a real musician's. It came as naturally as breathing, and the notes seemed to form in his head without any effort. For the first time in his life Richard was able to sit back and listen to himself play as though he were someone else. And he was better than he thought!

Richard noticed that the crowd returned when he came to the second page. But this time he wasn't so scared, and he had Skinny's backup behind him. He kept on right through the third page and back to the first, and when they reached the last measure, he didn't want to stop. So he flipped back to the beginning again.

They continued to play for nearly an hour, improvising and running circles around the simple melody. The ghost and Richard traded off leading until the boy's fingers were nearly cut through. Then it was over.

The applause was thunderous and dimmed slowly with the spectral audience.

"Whew!" whispered Skinny as the crowd faded. "You got real promise."

Richard held his guitar and breathed deeply. It was weird. It was too weird. But he felt great.

"You play like that and you'll win that show!" Skinny yelled.

But Richard shook his head.

"If I play by myself, I'll screw up. I get all nervous."

Skinny looked at the boy very seriously.

"You *still* think you need a backup?"

Richard's eyes lit up. "Maybe you could—"

"Wait a minute, kid. I can't leave this place. I've helped a lot of players in this club. But I can't leave."

"Why?" asked Richard desperately.

The ghost looked away. "I was the bartender in this joint. But I never had the guts to try to make it as a musician. I always wanted to, but I was too worried about not having a steady job. On the road, out there, you could end up like those other broken-hearted musicians. No money. No home. No nothing. So I only played in here after hours, when everyone was gone."

Richard stared at the oddly human ghost.

"I kept my guitar hidden under those steps so no one would know about it."

"You kept your playing a secret for your whole life?"

"Even my wife never knew about my dreams. Guess I was too scared of making a fool of myself. Anyway, that's why I haunt this place."

"So you can play for someone?"

"Right. But to play out there . . . I don't know."

"Why not?" asked Richard, knowing that with Skinny's playing behind him he could do anything.

"If I left, I would have to go someplace else . . . and I'm not sure I'm ready."

"What do you mean?"

"If I leave here, I have to go. You know, the big G-O. Gone, like dead and gone."

"I guess that's even scarier than my stupid stage fright," answered Richard.

Skinny didn't say anything.

There was a long pause, and the ghost looked as though he were trying to figure out the greatest riddle in the world. Then he suddenly pointed to the stairs. "You could take my guitar. It's still there under the steps."

"Are you sure?"

The specter nodded.

"You take it. Maybe I can't come myself, but my guitar might bring you some courage."

Richard frowned. He was sure he needed more than the old guitar. He needed a backup.

"You're good enough," insisted Skinny. "In fact, it would be terrible if you didn't play."

"You mean the same way you never did?"

The ghost looked hurt, yet he didn't argue.

"Just try it," replied Skinny with a sad smile.

Richard agreed, but it was clear that he hadn't gotten the answer he needed. He watched as Skinny faded into the darkness, and noticed an apprehensive scowl cross the old ghost's face just before he was gone.

There were at least two thousand people in the school auditorium, waiting for Richard to take his turn. He had spent all that morning in his room, practicing on Skinny's Gibson, but he still wasn't ready. His body was shaking so violently he could barely hold the big guitar. Stomach churning, Richard walked out and stared down at the boards of the stage. He felt his knees getting weak. Sweat was running down his back.

He was praying for a miracle. More than anything, he was hoping that Skinny had changed his mind and would show up. But as he sat down, all he could see was the eyes of the crowd staring back at him.

Richard adjusted the guitar and set his hands on the frets. He swallowed hard and told himself he was good enough. But he still didn't believe it. He still needed someone behind him.

Then, out of the corner of his eye, he saw it. In the back, hidden in the folds of the stage curtains, was a dark image—a very faint silhouette of a thin man holding a guitar like the one in Richard's hands.

Richard's heart leaped with delight. He wasn't alone.

The crowd hushed as Richard adjusted his seat and steadied himself. His fingers tensed, and he kept his eyes down so that he wouldn't remember the people watching him.

"You came," he whispered.

"I'm with you," replied the ghost. "I figured if you were brave enough to come out here by yourself, I better do what I should have done years ago. But I don't have much time, so let's go. One, two . . ."

The notes from Richard's guitar sang sweetly as he kept up with Skinny's style. The ghostly music filled his ears, and soon he was lost in the song and playing for sheer joy. The old Gibson rang out "After You've Gone" without a single lost note. It was so good, the whole auditorium began to swing with the haunting melody.

By the second repeat Richard had completely forgotten where he was, and the tune was flowing out of his very soul. Then, around the tenth measure on the second time around, he heard Skinny's voice again in his ear.

He was so exhilarated, he didn't really notice what the ghost was saying.

"You got it from here, kid," said Skinny softly. "I got to go."

Richard didn't hear when the ghost's music stopped. He was too much into the song and played right through to the end with style and flair. It was only as he finished that he realized he had carried the last verse by himself.

Then he looked at the audience, which leaped to its feet and began to cheer wildly. Apparently, no one had heard Skinny. No one except, possibly, Mr. Smentz. His teacher smiled and wiped a tear from his eye as Richard took an awkward bow. They looked at each other and then glanced at the ceiling to say good-bye to Skinny and his glorious music.

At the end of the show Richard brought the first-prize trophy backstage while his principal received the school's grant from the talent-show committee.

Richard's mother and Mr. Smentz were behind the curtains waiting for him. They applauded as he carried the large bronze cup and the old ghost's guitar into the wings.

"You were terrific," said his mom. "But whose guitar is that?"

"I think it's a gift," explained Mr. Smentz. "I know the man he got it from, and he won't need it anymore. He's gotten a much better instrument."

They both looked at the boy proudly.

"Here's your key," replied Richard. "I hope you aren't mad that Skinny's gone."

His mother seemed confused, but Mr. Smentz grinned broadly as he looked at his pupil and Skinny's old Gibson. "It's about time he moved on to a better club. We all have to do that at some point. Besides, I'll bet the crowd really liked your playing," replied the old man. "And there aren't many guitarists left who can play 'After You've Gone' like that . . . even fewer now. Maybe you could play for them again sometime?"

His mother thought Mr. Smentz was talking about the crowd in the auditorium, but Richard knew what he meant. As he put the key back in his pocket, both he and Mr. Smentz thought they heard a sweet tune playing in the distance. It was a happy melody that rolled off the frets of an ancient six-string, and they knew that Skinny was out there somewhere—and that he was playing better than ever.

This house isn't big enough for the both of us.

THE TENANT WHO FRIGHTENED A GHOST

Jessica Amanda Salmonson

Harriet Leichman did not believe in ghosts before she saw the pale stranger in her new house. "What are you doing here?" she shouted angrily. The young man turned slowly to face her. He replied, "Why, madam, I live here. I always have."

"Who are you?" she quizzed, and he said, "A ghost."

As she could see through him, she believed him right away, but she wasn't at all afraid. It seemed to Harriet that he was a mild-mannered and polite fellow. All the same, she did not see that she wanted to share her home with anyone else, not even a ghost.

Overcome by a sudden willfulness, she told the ghost a lie: "By a surprising coincidence, I am a ghost also."

"Is that so?" he said, raising his pale brow. Then he added: "Quite a few people have moved in here, then out again, frightened of me. Since the landlord has unknowingly rented to a ghost this time, I suppose I needn't worry about scaring you away."

"You have absolutely nothing to worry about on that score," said Harriet. "However, I happen to be an evil spirit and do startling things with no reason at all. I bite people's ears, kick them in the pants, and make spooky noises all night long. I've even been known to lift people into the air and drop them out of windows. It comes naturally, and I cannot control my urges. In fact, I'm not at all certain it will be safe for you from now on."

The mild and honest ghost looked hugely upset. "As for me," he said, "I have never hurt anyone and would not care to start. It sounds frightful to share my home with an evil spirit such as yourself. If you'll forgive me, I'm moving out."

The ghost soon vanished and was never seen again.

How many times can one ghost die?

SOUL SURVIVOR

Neal Shusterman

What I tell you now you can never tell another living soul.

It began as a dream—or what I thought was a dream. I was floating—rising higher and higher. Then, when I looked back, I could see someone lying in bed. It was a boy. Not just any boy—it was my own self, and I was lying in the stillness of sleep.

This was one of those dreams where you know you're dreaming—where you have your whole mind, not just part of it, to think things through and make sense of everything. An out-of-body experience—that's what they call it. And as it turns out, I picked just the wrong time to have one.

The room I was floating in was bright and clear, because dawn had already broken, and light was pouring in through the blinds. Then

I heard a noise growing louder. I should have realized something was wrong by the way it sounded. It grated against the silence of the morning, but I was so wrapped up in floating around the room, I didn't notice until it was too late.

There was a mighty roar and a shattering of wood and metal. Then something hot and silver passed through me, and in an instant it was gone.

So was my body.

So was the entire second story of our house.

A moment later, the blast of a great explosion shook the air.

When we had first moved to this house, my parents had asked me if I wanted the bedroom upstairs or downstairs. I had chosen upstairs. Big mistake. With the second floor of the house torn away, I could see my parents below in their roofless bedroom, screaming. They weren't hurt. No, they were terrified—still not knowing what had happened, and not understanding why there was morning sky above them instead of their ceiling fan.

But I knew exactly what had happened. A jumbo jet had taken off half of our house just before slamming into the ground two streets away.

As for my body, well, I'm sure it felt no pain because it was over so quickly. Anyway, I wouldn't know because I wasn't there to feel it. Perhaps if it hadn't happened so quickly, I might have been drawn back into my body to die with it, but that's not what happened.

Now I'm alive, but with no body to live in.

Perhaps that's how ghosts are made.

I remember drifting into school the next day, going up to my friends and screaming into their faces that I was still here. But they couldn't see me or hear me. I also remember hovering among the flowers at my funeral, thinking that being there was the proper and respectable thing to do.

For many weeks after that, I drifted through the rooms of my uncle's house, where my parents were staying now that our house was destroyed. I stayed there, sitting on the couch and watching TV with them. I sat on an empty chair at the dinner table, day after day, yet they never knew I was there . . . and never would.

Soon my parents' grief was too much for me to bear. There was nothing I could ever do to comfort them. So I left.

You can't imagine what it's like to have lost everything. Losing your house, and your things, and your friends, and your family is all bad enough—but to lose yourself along with it—*that* was beyond imagination. To lose my thick head of hair that I never liked to brush. To lose those fingernails that I still had the urge to bite. To lose the feeling of waking up to the warm sun on your face. To lose the taste of a cold drink, and the feel of a hot shower. To just *be,* with no flesh to contain your mind and soul. It was not a fun way to be.

I drifted to the lonely basement of an old abandoned building, and lay there for weeks, not wanting to go anywhere, not wanting to face a world I could not be part of. I just wanted to stay in that lonely place forever.

Perhaps that's how buildings become haunted.

It was months before I could bring myself to look upon the light of day again, and when I did, it was like coming out of a cocoon. Once I could accept that my old life was gone, I began to realize that I did have some sort of future, and I was ready to explore it.

I began by testing my speed. I was just an invisible, weightless spirit of the air, but I could will myself to move very fast. I practiced, building my skill of flight the way I had built my swimming speed in the pool—back in the days when I was flesh and bone. It wasn't that different, really, except now I didn't need muscles to make myself move, only thoughts.

Soon I could outrace the fastest birds and fly higher than the highest jets. I could turn on a dime and crash through solid rock as if I were diving through water. These were times I did not miss the heavy weight of my body.

And, wow—were there ever places to explore! I dove through the oceans, and actually moved through the belly of a great white shark. I dipped into the mouth of a volcano, racing through its dark stone cap—right into red-hot magma! I plunged deeper still, beyond the earth's mantle to hit its super-dense core. It wasn't as easy to move through as water and air, but I did it. I did all of these things!

And each time I would slip into one of these great and magical realms, I would play a game with myself.

"I am this mountain," I would say. Then I would expand myself like a cloud of smoke, until I could feel my whole spirit filling up the entire mountain—from the trees at its base, to the snow on its peak.

"I am this ocean," I would say. Then I would spread across the surface of the water, stretching myself from continent to continent.

"I am this planet," I would tell myself, stretching out in all directions until I could feel myself hurtling through space, caught in orbit around the sun.

But soon the game lost its joy, for try as I might, I could never stay in the place where I had put myself. I did not want to be a mountain, immense and solitary, moving only when the earth shook. I did not want to be a sea, rolling uneasily toward eternity, a slave of the moon and its tides. I did not want to be the earth, alone and spinning in an impossibly vast universe.

And so I dared to do something I hadn't found the nerve to do before. I began to move within the minds of human beings.

Like anything else, it took practice.

When I first slipped inside a human being, all I could see was the blood pumping through thousands of veins and arteries. All I could hear was the thump of a heartbeat. But soon I would settle within someone and begin to pick out a thought or two. And soon after that, I could hear all of that person's thoughts. Then I began to feel things the way that person felt them, and see the world through that person's eyes—without ever letting on that I was there.

It was almost like being human, and this hint of being human again drove me on with a determination I'd never felt before.

After many weeks of secretly dipping into people's minds, I discovered I could not only hear the thoughts of these people, but change those thoughts. I could make them turn left instead of right. I could make them have a sudden craving for an ice-cream sundae. Have you ever had a thought that seemed to come flying out of nowhere?

Perhaps someone was passing through you.

I moved daily from person to person, taking bits of knowledge with me as I went, taking memories of lives I'd never lived. I got to dive off cliffs in Mexico, experience the excitement and terror of being born, and I even blasted into space in a rocket, hiding deep within the mind of an astronaut.

This was a game I could have enjoyed forever . . . if I hadn't gotten so good at it. You see, I came way too close to the minds on which I hitchhiked.

"Who are you?"

The voice came as a complete surprise to me. I didn't know what to do.

"Who are you?" he demanded. "And why are you in my head?"

I was in the mind of a baseball player. I'd been there for a few weeks, and this was the first time he'd spoken to me.

He was a rookie named Sam "Slam" McKellen—I'm sure you've heard of him. They called him Slam because of the way he blasted balls right out of the stadium at least once a game. I know because I swung the bat with him.

"You'd better answer me," his thoughts demanded.

McKellen was the first one to know I was there. I was thrilled . . . but also terrified.

"My name is Peter," I said, and then I told him about the plane crash. I explained how I had lost my body, and how I had survived for more than a year on my own. I must have gone on babbling for hours—it was the first time I had someone to talk to.

McKellen listened to all I had to tell him, sitting quietly in a chair. Then, when I was done, he did something amazing. He asked me to stay.

"We have batboys in the dugout to help us out," he told me. "Who says I can't have a batboy on the *inside* as well? Heck, I'm important enough." He began to smile. "Sure," he said, "someone to pick up my stray thoughts that happen to wander off. Someone to remind me when I'm late, or when I forget something important. Sure, stay, kid," he said. "Stay as long as you want."

I don't need to tell you how it changed my life. It's not everyone who gets to live inside a major league baseball player. I mean, I was with Slam every time he swung that bat, every time he raced around those bases, every time he slid into home. And when he came up to accept his MVP trophy that year—it was *our* hands that held it in the air.

When we went out to eat, sometimes he

would let me take over, giving me total control of his body. That way *I* could be the one feeding us that hot-fudge sundae—and tasting every last bit of it.

At night we would have long conversations about baseball and the nature of the universe—a silent exchange of thoughts from his mind to mine. In fact, we did this so often our thoughts were beginning to get shuffled, and I didn't know which were his thoughts and which were mine. Pretty soon I figured our two sets of thoughts and memories would blend together forever, like two colors of paint. As far as I was concerned, that would be just fine.

But then one day he offered to do something for me that I never had the nerve to ask him to do, and it changed everything.

"I'm gonna write your parents a letter," he announced. "I'm gonna tell them that you're alive and well and living inside my head."

I should have realized how that letter would have sounded, but I was too thrilled by the offer to think about what might happen. So we wrote the letter together and mailed it. Then, three days later, the world came collapsing down around us like a dam in a flood.

You see, my parents were never much for believing anything they couldn't see with their own eyes. When they got the letter, they called the police. The police called the newspapers, and suddenly the season's star MVP was a nutcase who heard voices.

Sam "Slam" McKellen became the overnight laughingstock of the American League. It's funny how that happens sometimes . . . but it wasn't funny to us.

I tried to get him to shut up, but he insisted on telling it like it is, getting up in front of the microphones and explaining to the world how a kid was renting space in his brain. We even went to see my parents, and although I kept feeding him facts about my past that only I could know, my parents were still convinced McKellen was a madman.

We were sent to doctors. Then we were put in hospitals and filled with so much medication, that sometimes it seemed like there was a whole platoon of us in there, not just two.

In the end Slam finally broke.

"Peter, I want you to leave," he told me as we sat alone in the dark, in the big house our baseball contract had bought. Our hair was uncombed and our face had been unshaved for weeks.

"The doctors are right," Slam announced. "You don't exist, and I won't share my mind with someone who does not exist."

I could hardly believe what I was hearing.

"I order you to leave and never come back," he said. "Never look for me. Never talk to me.

Never come near my thoughts again." And then he began to cry. "I hate you!" he screamed—not just in our head, but out loud. "I hate you for what you've done to me!"

I could have left then. I could have run away to find someone else who wouldn't mind sharing his life with a poor dispossessed soul like myself. But I realized that I didn't want to leave.

And I didn't want to share anymore, either.

"I'm not leaving," I told him. "*You* are."

That's how the battle began.

A tug of war between two minds in one brain is not a pretty sight. On the outside our face turned red, and our eyes went wild. Our legs and arms began convulsing as if we were having an epileptic fit.

On the inside we were screaming—battling each other with thoughts and fury. His inner words came swinging at me like baseball bats. But I withstood the blows, sending my own angry thoughts back like an iron fist, pounding down on him. Yes, I smashed that thankless baseball player with my ironfisted thoughts again and again, until I could feel myself gaining control. This was my body now. Not his. Not his ever again.

I pounded and pounded on his mind and filled his brain until there was no room for him anymore. But try as I might, I could not push him out. I could only push him *down.* So I pushed him down until the great baseball player was nothing more than a tremor in my right hand.

I had control of everything else . . . but even that wasn't good enough. As long as any part of him was still there, he could come back, and I didn't want that. I had to figure out a way to get rid of him—for *good.*

That's when I remembered the dolphins.

In all my travels through air, land, and sea, there was only one place I knew I had to stay away from.

The mind of the dolphin.

I came close to the mind of a dolphin once. I had thought I might slip one on for size—but the place is *huge*! A dolphin's brain is larger than a human's, and its mind is like an endless maze of wordless thought.

When I had first neared a dolphin, I had felt myself being pulled into that mind, as if it were a black hole. I resisted, afraid I would get lost in there—*trapped* in there, wandering forever through a mind too strange to fathom.

And so I had turned away from the creature before I had been caught in its unknowable depths.

But now I had to find a dolphin again.

With the baseball player's spirit still making my hand quiver, I made a two-hundred-mile trek to Ocean World—a great marine park where they had countless dolphins in captivity.

The whole time I didn't dare sleep, sure that the baseball player would fight his way back in control of my new body.

I arrived at midnight. A full moon was out and the empty parking lot was like a great black ocean.

With the strong body of the athlete I possessed, I climbed the fence and made my way to the dolphin tanks.

The plan was simple—I had worked it out a dozen times on my way there, and I knew that nothing could go wrong. I was stronger than the baseball player—I had already proven that. All that remained was getting him out of this body forever. Then, and only then, would it truly be mine.

I held on to that thought as I dove into the frigid water of the dolphin tank. Then, as I began to sink, I let Slam climb back into my mind. He was crazed now, screaming in anger and fear. He did not know what I was about to do, because I had kept my thoughts from him.

Suddenly there was a dolphin swimming up to us. It appeared to be just curious as to what was going on in its tank. As it drew near, and nearer still, I waited. Then when it was right up next to us, I blasted the baseball player out of my mind.

Though I'd tried many times to do that, this time it wasn't hard at all. In fact, it was as easy as blowing a feather out of my hand—because

KEE
OUT

this time there was a place for his spirit to go. It went into the dolphin . . . and there it stayed.

But the dolphin clearly did not want that kind of company. It began to swim around the huge tank, bucking and twisting as if it could shed this new spirit that had merged with its own. But the dolphin's efforts were useless. Slam was now a permanent resident in the dolphin's mind.

And as for me—I was free! I was the sole owner of this fine body! All I had to do was swim back to the surface to begin my new life.

All I had to do was swim.

All I had to do . . .

That's when I discovered that this strong athletic body, this body that had hit a hundred fastballs over the right-field wall . . . had never learned to swim.

Slowly panic set in. I moved my hands, I kicked my legs, but the muscles in my body had no memory of how to behave in water. They thrashed uselessly back and forth, and my lungs filled with the icy water. Meanwhile the dolphin swam furiously around the tank, not caring about me or my new body, but trying to find the foreign spirit that had entered its mind.

I felt death begin to pound in my ears with the heavy beat of my slowing heart, and I knew that if I didn't leave this body soon, it would be too late.

I had to leap out of it. I *had* to give it up. If I stayed in this body a few minutes longer, I might not have been able to escape it—I might have been bound to it the way normal people are bound to their bodies. But my will was strong, and my skill at body-jumping well honed.

And so I tore myself from my new body, letting my spirit float to the surface like a buoy . . . while there, at the bottom of the dolphin tank, the soulless body of the great baseball player drowned.

I don't know what happened after that, because I left and didn't look back. I have heard tales, though, of a dolphin who leaped out of its tank so often that they had to put a fence over it. But who knows if stories like that are ever true?

And that brings me to you.

You see, I've been with you longer than you think. I've been sitting on your shoulder watching what you do, what you say, and even how you say it. I know the names of your relatives. I know your friends. We've already shared several hot-fudge sundaes together.

And if someday very soon, you wake up only to find yourself walking toward a dolphin pool in the dead of night . . . don't worry.

Because I know you can swim.

It takes a real bonehead to dis the fish!

SHARK!

John Gregory Betancourt

Jake and me were walking along the rusted old railroad tracks to the back of Old Man Cooper's farm when it happened.

It was one of them perfect summer days, hot and sunny and bright. Crickets *brr*ed loudly in the tall weeds around us. It must've been a hundred degrees out, and we'd both tied our T-shirts around our waists to feel the sun on our backs. The air smelled of hot grass and baking earth and cow manure from the dairy pasture up ahead.

We'd been hunting for fossils in the embankment where the railroad cut through a low hill, like we did every summer. Jake had found a black shark's tooth as long as his little finger there last summer, but though we'd searched for more ever since, we hadn't found any. Today all we saw were broken bits of shells.

Jake was my best friend. We were both twelve. I was a couple months older, but he was three inches taller. It was August and the middle of summer vacation. I couldn't think of a better way to spend it than with Jake. His father was off building houses in Goldfield County, and my pa didn't need me to help out at his dry-goods store except on weekends, so we were on our own and out exploring.

Suddenly I heard a low roar, like a swarm of bees. Three kids on mopeds burst through the weeds and scrub on top of the embankment to our left. They came whizzing down and across the tracks inches away from us, laughing, revving their motors, trying to scare us. One had a skull on the front of his helmet, one had a giant black bat, and one had lightning bolts. All three had dark visors down so we couldn't see their faces. I knew who they were, though. And so did Jake.

Jake picked up a fist-sized rock. "Get on out of here, Billy Trent!" he called. He held the rock like he meant to throw it. His freckled face had gone all hard, and his short brown hair bristled up in back like a porcupine.

I picked up a rock, too. Billy Trent was our class bully. He'd been held back two grades, so he was older than us, and he liked to push everyone around because of it. Holding him back hadn't made him smarter. It had just made him meaner.

"Dweebs!" Billy laughed behind his skull helmet. Then he skidded his rear wheel, spraying us with loose gravel, and went roaring up the other side of the embankment. The other two bikers raced after him. I listened until the sound of their motors faded in the distance.

Jake relaxed. "He wasn't looking for a fight today, I guess," he said. Then he stared at the rock in his hand. "Hey, look at this, Davy!"

"What?"

"It's a bone!"

I leaned over to see. It looked like part of the backbone of a fish . . . a big fish, something twenty or thirty times larger than the rainbow trout Pa brought home from Piedmont Lake.

"I bet it's from the shark," I said enviously. I began scouting around where he'd found it. "Do you think there's more?"

"Yes!" he said. "Look at these!" He pulled two more pieces of bone out of the earth. They had looked like rocks to me. But now that I knew what to look for, I could tell they were shark bones, too.

I scouted around and finally found one, and he found another. Suddenly we were both pulling out pieces of fossil backbone. They seemed to be scattered over a thirty-foot area beside the railroad tracks. We laid them out on the ground beside the tracks as we hunted, setting larger next to smaller, fitting one to another. It wasn't real hard; all the backbones went in a straight line, and you just had to arrange them in the right order. Nothing so complicated as a real dinosaur, like the T Rex they had in the Natural History Museum we visited last year on our class trip.

We worked feverishly, hardly able to believe our luck. An hour and a half later the fossil shark stretched out nearly seven feet long. It would have been even longer, but a couple of the bones were missing. The last thing Jake found was part of the jaw, a good eight-inch section of it, complete with a triangular black tooth as long as my thumb. The tooth Jake had found last summer matched it exactly. The bones had all eroded from the embankment, I thought, and tumbled down here long ago.

"How long do you think the skeleton's been here?" I asked.

"A million years, I bet," he said solemnly.

"Mr. Deering will know." He was our science teacher. "We can ask him when school starts."

"I bet," Jake said, "the shark got buried alive in some ancient disaster. He's been trying to get out ever since."

"And we found him," I said proudly.

"And put him back together," he added. He

had a funny look in his eye. "He's going to be grateful. He *owes* us."

"That's dumb," I said.

He shot me a quick glance, then grinned. "Yeah, it is, isn't it? Come on, let's get him back home."

He untied his shirt and spread it out; then we began piling the bones on top of it. It would be a heavy load, but we could manage it between us.

Finding a shark was the coolest thing I'd ever done in my life. When everyone at school found out, we'd be famous. Maybe we'd even get our pictures in the paper.

Before we had finished, though, I heard the roar of mopeds again. It was Billy Trent and his friends. They were racing along the railroad tracks somewhere off to our left.

When they burst around the bend and saw us, Jake and I froze, staring. They weren't going to stop, I realized. They were going to run us down.

I pulled Jake into the tall weeds beside the tracks, scattering dragonflies and grasshoppers. The mopeds zipped past two feet away.

Billy Trent circled back and pulled up where we'd been working. He nudged Jake's T-shirt with the toe of his Reebok.

"What's this?" he asked.

"Bones," I told him. "They're ours. We found 'em."

"Not anymore, they're not." He ripped Jake's shirt from under the bones and threw it in his face. "Clear off. This is our territory."

"It's railroad property—" Jake began hotly.

I caught his arm and pulled him back. Sometimes he didn't know when to back down.

"There's three of them," I whispered.

"So?" he demanded.

"So I'm not going to fight over a few old bones!"

Jake set his jaw stubbornly and made fists. "They're *our* bones. They're *special.*"

"Are you crazy?" I whispered. "What can they do to them? They'll leave 'em here. Play it cool, we can get them later."

He hesitated. I knew he wasn't looking forward to fighting. I'd seen him fight like a devil when he had to, and he might have taken Billy Trent alone. They were almost the same height, after all, and Jake was pretty strong. But I wasn't much of a fighter, and Billy's two friends tipped the odds pretty far against us. They would have pounded us both to jelly.

"All right," he finally said. He unclenched his fists, picked up his T-shirt, and stomped up the embankment through the weeds. I followed right on his heels.

Behind us Billy and his friends began to cluck like chickens. I felt my face and neck turning beet red, but I didn't look back. If I had, I would've lost it and gotten the stuffing pounded out of me. So much for playing it cool.

Jake wouldn't go home after that. "I want to know what they're doing," he insisted when we were out of their sight.

"All right," I said. I didn't see how that could hurt.

We circled around and came up on the embankment at a different spot. There we peeked through the weeds.

Billy and the other two had parked their mopeds and taken off their helmets. Billy had shoulder-length blond hair, a narrow face, and tiny, piglike eyes. One of the others, a lanky kid with red hair, I recognized as his cousin Jerry. I didn't know the third kid, who had long black hair tied in a ponytail. Probably another cousin. Billy was the kind of kid only relatives liked.

"Watch this one!" Billy cried. He picked up the biggest piece of backbone, about the size of a softball, and heaved it as hard as he could. It went over the other side of the embankment. I couldn't see how far it went or where it landed.

Beside me Jake gave a low moan. "A million years," he whispered.

"We'll find the pieces later," I whispered back.

"It took him a million years to get put back together, and look what happens. How can they break him up like that?"

We watched for fifteen minutes while they threw bones and hooted and called to one another. When only the jawbone remained, Billy smashed it on the railroad tracks until it broke into a lot of tiny pieces, then threw the pieces into the air as high as he could. They landed in the tallest patch of weeds.

Whooping and hollering, he put his helmet back on, jumped onto his moped, and began pedaling. The others joined him. In seconds they had their motors roaring. Then they were gone.

Jake and I stood. I felt numb inside.

"Why'd they have to do that?" Jake said to himself. He looked pale—sick, almost.

"Oh, come on, it's no big deal," I said to try to cheer him up. "We'll see how many pieces we can find."

I ran down to the tracks and began poking around in the weeds for the jawbone Billy had smashed, since that was the closest piece. Maybe the tooth could be saved.

He joined me. We couldn't find the tooth. Then we spread out and searched for the backbones. We couldn't find them, either—not even one. When it began to get dark an hour or so later, we still hadn't found a single bone. It was as if they'd vanished from the face of the earth.

"A million years," I heard Jake muttering several times to himself. "He waited a million years, and this is what he gets. Someone needs to teach that Billy Trent a lesson."

"Well, it's not going to be us," I said. "We belong to the chicken club, remember?"

He gave me a strange look. "I'm no chicken."

"Yeah. But you're not a shark, either," I said, trying to make it into a joke.

I got home too late for supper, but Ma had saved me a plate of roast beef and a couple of biscuits. I wolfed it down as I told her about the shark bones and what Billy Trent had done with them.

"I'm proud of you," she said. "A few old bones aren't worth fighting over."

"Yeah," I said. But I remembered Jake's face and knew he didn't feel that way. He was always getting too caught up in stuff. "How old do you think that shark was?"

"Well," she said slowly, wiping her hands on her apron, "I don't know. But I reckon a million years sounds about right. It's been a long time since there's been sharks hereabouts, at least the swimming kind."

We both laughed about that. Pa liked to call bankers "sharks" sometimes.

"Do you think you should tell somebody about the shark?" she went on.

"Who?"

"I don't know . . . the police? Scientists, maybe? Experts of some kind?"

"When Davy found that big tooth last year, Mr. Deering said that whatever fossils you find, you get to keep. That's the law. He did a whole class on local fossils, and we all went out hunting, remember?"

"I guess . . . ," she said. I could tell she didn't remember Mr. Deering's fossil-hunting expedition, though.

"Yep," I said wistfully, leaning back in my seat. "That shark would've been *ours.*"

Later that night, as I lay in bed, I stared out my open window. The full moon shone on the neatly plowed fields next door. Farther off, I could see lights from Clinton Corners, where Pa had his store. It was hard to imagine all this land being under water, with fish and such swimming about.

I'd once seen a National Geographic special about sharks. They were supposed to be just about the meanest predators of all time. Whoever made that show hadn't met Billy Trent, I thought with a grin. Predators came in all shapes and sizes these days.

I began to imagine we were under water and it was a million years ago. As I drifted to sleep, I thought I saw a great white shark swimming slowly past my window. It seemed to be smiling.

* * *

I awakened to my father's voice calling me. It was past dawn. I'd slept later than usual. I hoped breakfast wouldn't be too cold; my mother always cooked early since Pa had to be at the store by seven o'clock.

"Coming!" I called, jumping out of bed. "Save me some bacon!" I pulled on a clean T-shirt and shorts, slipped on my Nikes, and sprinted downstairs.

Leroy Cobb, the county sheriff, was standing in the kitchen, sipping a mug of Ma's coffee. I stopped and stared. He was in his brown uniform, wearing his gun at his side, and he wasn't smiling. And neither were my parents.

"Where were you last night, son?" the sheriff asked.

"Right here," I said, a lump forming in my throat. "Why?"

"Well, Billy Trent is missing, and someone took what looks like a chain saw to his bike. I found it out by I-65. I understand from his cousins you and he had a little run-in yesterday."

"Uh-huh." I looked at my mother, who nodded for me to continue. So I told the sheriff all that had happened. The only thing I left out was the chicken noises Billy and his friends had made when Jake and I slunk off with our tails between our legs.

He nodded gravely when I finished. "Do you recognize this?" he asked.

He opened his hand. Lying in his palm was a triangular black shark's tooth. It looked exactly like the one Jake had in the jar in his bedroom . . . and exactly like the one we'd found yesterday.

"It looks like a shark's tooth," I said.

"It was buried in the rubber of one of his tires," he said.

"He must have picked it up when he was riding along the railroad tracks," I told him. "We had one just about like that yesterday, but he took it away from us." God, I sounded like a wimp. I couldn't even hang on to a shark's tooth!

"Well, if you can think of anything else you want me to know, give me a call," he said.

"Yes, sir."

He finished his coffee, thanked my ma, nodded to my pa, and left. Pa watched him go, then sighed.

"It was Jake, wasn't it?" he said.

"I don't know," I said truthfully.

He was awfully mad yesterday, I thought . . . and if anyone in our class could have taken Billy Trent in a fair fight, it was him.

"Billy Trent's probably holed up somewhere licking his wounds," Pa said, "trying to get everyone worried. But two wrongs don't make a right. Got me?"

"Yes, sir," I said.

"I don't expect any more visits from the sheriff," he went on.

"But I didn't—" I caught his look. "Yes, sir."

Ma was making pancakes. I sat and waited, sipping my milk. Finally she set a stack in front of me. I gobbled them up, excused myself, then lit out of there for Jake's house at a run.

The sheriff had already been there when I arrived. Jake's mother sent me up to his room.

I found him sitting on his bed staring thoughtfully out the window. He was swinging his feet a bit. He looked a lot happier than he had late yesterday.

"Jake," I said.

"Davy," he replied.

"The sheriff had a tooth."

"I saw it."

"It looked familiar," I said.

"Yep."

I sat beside him. "Well?" I finally asked.

"I didn't do it," he said. Then he grinned. "But I wish I had!"

"Jake . . ."

"And if I did, do you think I'd be stupid enough to leave a shark tooth?"

"Well . . ." I hesitated. It *didn't* make a lot of sense. "I guess not," I said.

"The sheriff said maybe a truck hit his bike.

Maybe Billy abandoned it by I-65. He didn't know. There wasn't any blood or anything."

"What about that tooth, though?"

Jake got up, went to his desk, and picked up his jar. He hesitated a moment, then threw it to me.

Something rattled inside. I held it up to the light and saw a black shark's tooth through the yellow glass. The sheriff hadn't found Jake's tooth in the wheel, after all.

I bit my lip, confused. I would have bet cash that he'd done it. He'd always had a bad temper, and Billy had certainly riled him up good.

Jake was still grinning . . . still holding something back, I thought. I'd known him long enough to see it in his eyes.

"So?" I prompted.

"I have an idea who did it," he admitted.

"Who?"

"You're going to think it's crazy."

"I won't!"

"Promise?"

"I promise, already!" I said.

"The shark did it."

I laughed out loud. "It's just bones, Jake! They can't hurt anybody!"

"A million years of waiting," he said softly, "and he's free and put back together for all of half an hour before someone comes along and breaks him apart. You'd be mad, too, wouldn't you, Davy? *Wouldn't you?*"

I shivered a bit. I thought of the great white shark grinning outside my window last night. And then I thought of Billy Trent's shiny new moped, mangled forever by powerful jaws, and Billy missing. A shark like that could swallow a kid whole. And there *was* a tooth in the tire.

I'd been mistaken, I thought. Billy wasn't a real predator. He was nothing next to a shark.

"Yes," I said slowly, "I'd be mad, too."

They never did find any trace of Billy Trent. It was as though he'd vanished off the face of the earth, just like the shark bones. Most everyone thought he simply ran off. "He was a wild one," they'd say, shaking their heads. "He's probably in the city making trouble there by now." Every kid in our class at school felt relief.

As for me, I don't know what really happened, but I'm keeping an open mind. At night I sometimes stare into the sky and think about the shark. And when the moon is full and I'm almost asleep, I think I see it up there swimming among the stars. It's always grinning, like it has a full belly. And sometimes, when I listen real hard, I think I can still hear Billy Trent scream.

The ghost in Benjie Perkins' kitchen needs his help. Will he be able to rise to the occasion?

BISCUITS OF GLORY

Bruce Coville

I am haunted by biscuits—Elvira Thistledown's biscuits, to be more precise. But I don't have any regrets. If I had it to do over again, I would still eat one, if only to free that poor woman from her curse. I'd do it even knowing how it was going to affect the rest of my life.

I was ten when it happened. We had just moved into a new house. Well, new to us; it was really a very old one—the fifth we had been in that I could remember. That was how my parents made their living: buying old houses, fixing them up, then selling them for a bundle of money. It was sort of neat, except it meant we never stayed in any one place too long, the places we moved into were always sort of crummy, and just when they got good, we had to move on.

Anyway, on our third night in the house I heard a clatter in the kitchen. Now, all old houses have their noises, their own personal creaks and groans, and I was still getting used to the sounds of this house. But something about this particular noise didn't sound right to me. So I grabbed my baseball bat and headed for the stairs.

I grabbed the bat instead of waking my parents because I had been through this before. I was tired of embarrassing myself, so I generally investigated night noises on my own. But I always carried my trusty Louisville Slugger when I did. Just in case, you know?

The floor was cold against my feet.

My door squeaked as I opened it.

Trying not to wake my parents, I tiptoed along the hall, past the peeling wallpaper (roses the size of cabbages, floating against gray stripes—truly ugly), past the bathroom with its leaky faucets (I had already gotten used to *that* noise), on to the head of the stairs.

I paused and listened.

Something was definitely moving in the kitchen. I could hear scrapes and thumps, soft and gentle, but no less real for all that. I was about to go wake my parents after all, when I heard something else, something totally unexpected.

I heard a woman singing.

I leaned forward and closed my eyes (I don't know what good that was supposed to do, but you know how it is), straining to hear. The voice was soft, sweet and sad—almost like someone singing a hymn. I had to go halfway down the steps to make out the words:

Biscuits, biscuits of glory
This is my story,
Biscuits of glory . . .

By now the hair was standing up on the back of my neck. Yet somehow I didn't think anyone who sounded so sad and sweet could hurt me.

Clutching my Louisville Slugger, I tiptoed down the rest of the steps and stopped outside the kitchen door.

"Biscuits, biscuits of glory," sang the voice, sounding so sad I almost started to cry myself.

Pushing lightly on the kitchen door, I swung it open just a crack. When I peeked through, I let out a little squeak of fright. There was no one in sight, not a person to be seen.

What I did see was a bag of flour, which wouldn't have been that unusual, except for the fact that this bag was *floating* in mid-air.

"Biscuits of glory," sang the voice, as the bag of flour opened, seemingly by itself. "Lighter than lovin', floatin' to heaven, straight from my oven . . ."

Now a measuring cup floated into the air and dipped into the flour bag. A little thrill ran down my spine as the cup came out of the bag. Suddenly I could see the hand that was holding it. That was because the hand was now covered with flour.

The hand repeated the action. It was an eerie sight: a floating hand, seemingly unattached to anything else, dumping flour into a big ceramic bowl.

Next came the baking powder. *Lots* of baking powder.

"Biscuits, biscuits of glory . . . ," sang the ghost. Her voice caught as she choked back a sob.

I couldn't help myself. Stepping through the door into the kitchen, I said, "What is it? What's wrong?"

The flour-covered hand jerked sideways, knocking over the container of baking powder. "Who are you?" asked the ghost in a soft voice, almost as if *she* was frightened of *me*.

"I'm Benjie Perkins. I live here. Who are you?"

"Elvira Thistledown," whispered the voice, so lightly it was as if the words were floating. "I died here."

I shivered. "What are you doing?"

"Making biscuits," she replied, setting the baking powder upright once more. "I make biscuits every Saturday night. Saturday at midnight. It's my curse."

"Sort of a strange curse."

"It was a strange death," whispered the ghost of Elvira Thistledown, as her one visible hand picked up a fork and began to stir the flour.

"Care to talk about it?" I asked.

My mother had always said I was a good listener.

"I can talk while I work," she said.

Taking that to be a *yes,* I pulled up a stool and sat next to the counter. Soon I was so involved in her story, I stopped paying much attention to what she was doing. Oh, how I wish now that I had watched more carefully!

"I always loved to make biscuits," said Elvira Thistledown. "My mother taught me when I was only seven years old, and soon my daddy was saying that he thought I was the best biscuit maker in the county."

"You must have liked that."

"I did," she said, sounding happy for the first time since we had begun to talk.

"I hate to interrupt," I said, "but is it possible for you to become visible? I might feel less nervous if you did."

"Well, it's not easy. But you seem like a nice boy. Just a minute and I'll see what I can do."

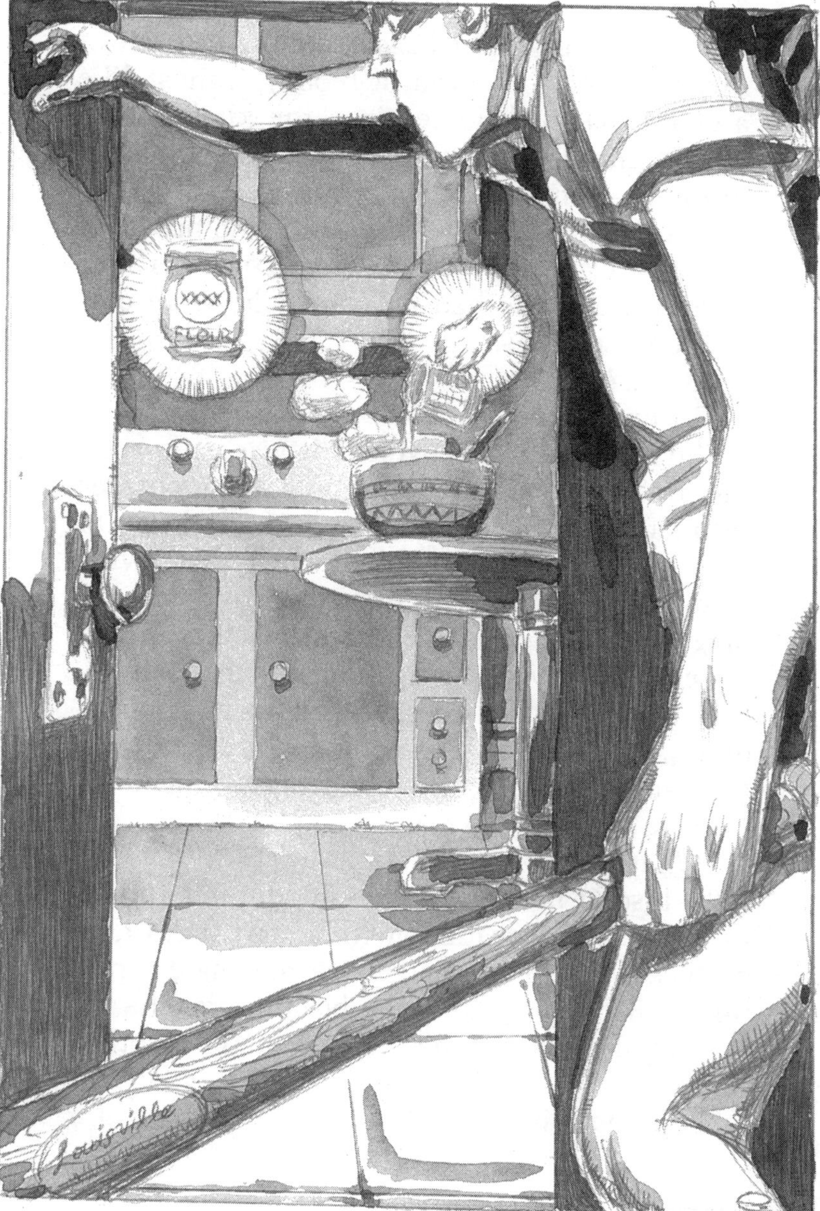
XXXX
FLOUR
Louisville

Soon a milky light began to glow in front of me. It started out kind of blobby, almost like a cloud that had floated into the kitchen, but after a minute or two it condensed into the form of a woman. She was younger and prettier than I had expected, with a turned-up nose and a long neck. I don't know what color her hair or eyes were; she had no color. She wore old-fashioned clothes.

"Better?"

"I think so."

She returned to her work. "It was vanity did me in," she said, measuring baking powder into the mix. "I was so proud of my biscuits that I just couldn't stand it when that awful Dan McCarty moved into town and started bragging that *he* made the best biscuits in the state. 'Why, my biscuits are lighter than dandelion fluff,' he used to say. 'Apt to float away on the first stiff breeze.' After a while his proud talk got to me, and I challenged him to a contest."

"What kind of a contest?"

"A biscuit bake-off," she said, dumping milk into the bowl. I realized with a start that I had no idea where she was getting her ingredients from. "Both of us to make biscuits, results to be judged by Reverend Zephyr of the Baptist Church."

"Did you win?"

She was busy working on her biscuits, so she didn't answer right away. She had turned the dough out onto the counter and was kneading it lightly. After a few minutes she began to pat it out to an even thickness. When it was about a half an inch thick, she turned to me and said in a bitter voice, "I lost. I lost, and that was the beginning of my downfall. I became obsessed with biscuits. I swore I would make a better biscuit than Dan McCarty or die trying."

Using the top of the baking-powder can, she began to cut the dough into rounds, flipping them off the counter and onto a baking sheet as she spoke.

"We began to have a weekly contest, Dan and I. Every Sunday morning we'd take our biscuits to church, and after the service Reverend Zephyr would try them out. He'd measure them. He'd weigh them. Finally he'd taste them, first plain, then with butter, then with honey. And every Sunday he'd turn to me and say, 'I'm sorry, Elvira, but Dan's biscuits are just lighter and fluffier than yours.' "

She popped the tray into the oven. "I was like a madwoman. I worked day and night, night and day, trying every combination I could think of to make my biscuits lighter, fluffier, more wonderful than any that had ever been made. I wanted biscuits that would float out of the oven and melt in your mouth. I wanted biscuits that would make a kiss seem heavy. I wanted biscuits that would make the angels weep with envy. I tried adding whipped egg whites, baking soda and vinegar, even yeast. But do too much of that, and you don't really have a biscuit anymore. No, the key is in the baking powder."

Her eyes were getting wild now, and I was beginning to be frightened again. I wondered if she really was crazy—and if she was, just what a crazy ghost might do.

"One Sunday I was sure I had it; I came to church with a basket of biscuits that were like a stack of tiny feather beds. But after the judging Reverend Zephyr shook his head sadly and said, 'I'm sorry, Elvira, but Dan's biscuits are just lighter and fluffier than yours.'

"By the next Saturday night I was wild, desperate, half-insane. In a fit of desperation I dumped an entire can of baking powder into my dough."

"What happened?" I asked breathlessly.

"The oven door blew off and killed me on the spot. And ever since, I've been doomed to bake a batch of biscuits every Saturday at midnight, as punishment for my pride. What's worse, I finally know the secret. Learned it on the other side. These biscuits are the lightest, fluffiest ever made, Benjie. Just plain heavenly.

But no one has ever tasted them, and I can't rest until someone does."

"How come no one has ever tasted them?"

"How can they? My biscuits of glory are so light and fluffy, they float right out of the oven and disappear through the ceiling. If I could leave them on the counter overnight, someone might have tried them by now. But they're always gone before anyone gets a chance."

She sounded like she was going to cry. "I'm so weary of biscuits," she sighed, "so everlastingly weary of baking biscuits. . . ."

"These biscuits of yours—they wouldn't hurt someone who ate them, would they?"

"Of course not!" she cried, and I could tell that I had offended her. "These are Biscuits of Glory. One bite and you'll never be the same."

"What if I grabbed one as it came out of the oven?"

"You'd burn your hand."

"Wait here!" I said.

Scooting out of the kitchen, I scurried up the stairs and rummaged through my room until I found what I was looking for—not easy, when you've just moved. Finally I located it. I went down the stairs two at a time, hoping to make it to the kitchen before Elvira's biscuits came out of the oven.

She was standing by the big old oven as I slipped through the swinging door.

"What's that?" she asked as I came in.

"My catcher's mitt. Are the biscuits ready?"

"They can't wait any longer," she replied. "They're done to perfection."

As she spoke, she opened the oven door. Out floated a dozen of the most perfect biscuits I had ever seen—light, golden-brown, high and fluffy, crusty around the edges. They escaped in sets of three, rising like the hot-air balloons at the state fair.

Reaching out with the mitt, I snagged a biscuit from the third set.

"Careful," said Elvira. "They're hot!"

Ignoring her warning, I took the biscuit from the glove. "Ow!" I cried as it slipped through my fingers and headed for the ceiling.

The last row of biscuits had already left the oven. I scrambled onto the counter and snagged one just as it was heading out of reach. I was more careful this time, cupping the glove over it and holding it tenderly while it cooled. I could feel the heat, but the leather protected me.

Finally I thought it was safe to try a bite. Elvira Thistledown watched with wide eyes as I took her work from my glove and lifted it to my lips.

It was astonishing—the most incredible biscuit I had ever tasted.

Suddenly I realized something even more astonishing: *I* was floating! I had lifted right off the counter and was hovering in midair. I worried about getting down, but as I chewed and swallowed, I drifted gently to the floor.

"What an amazing biscuit," I cried. "I feel like I've died and gone to heaven!"

"So do I!" said Elvira Thistledown. Only the last word was dragged out into an *Eye-eeeeeee. . . .*, as if she were being snatched into the sky.

That was the last I ever saw of Elvira Thistledown.

Her biscuits, however, haunt me still. It's not just the memory of their taste, though I have never again tasted anything so fine. It's the effect of the darn things. See, whenever I get too happy, or too excited, or begin thinking about those biscuits too much, I start to float. If I dream of them—and I often do—I may wake to find myself drifting a foot or two above the bed.

It gets a little embarrassing, sometimes.

I'll tell you this, though. Unlike some people, I'm not afraid of what happens after you die.

I know what I'll find waiting on the other side.

Biscuits of Glory.

ABOUT THE AUTHORS

MARY K. WHITTINGTON is the author of *The Patchwork Lady* and other picture books, and fantasy and spooky short stories for young people. She lives in Kirkland, Washington, and teaches writing and music to kids and adults.

LAWRENCE WATT-EVANS is the author of some two dozen novels as well as about a hundred short stories, including several in this series. He invented George Pinkerton for a series of bed-time stories for his own kids, and is pleased to share him with a larger audience.

JULIE EVANS prints her own money legally from time to time in her job at the Bureau of Engraving and Printing, but doesn't bring her work home with her. She has written several humorous articles and collaborated on a few short stories.

NANCY VARIAN BERBERICK lives in Charlotte, North Carolina, with her husband, Bruce A. Berberick, and their dog, Pagie. Nancy writes fantasy novels and short stories for grown-ups. Her work has appeared in the *Dragonlance* series.

GREG LABARBERA lives in Charlotte, North Carolina, with his wife, Jackie, and their three black Labradors. When he's not writing, Greg teaches elementary school physical education.

JOHN GREGORY BETANCOURT is the author of eleven science-fiction and fantasy novels, including two best-selling *Star Trek* books. He also runs a publishing company, Wildside Press, with his wife, and works on novels based on films and television shows such as *Lois & Clark: The New Adventures of Superman.*

MEL GILDEN is the author of over thirty middle-grade and young adult books, including the *My Brother Blubb* series, and several novels for adults, including two *Star Trek: Deep Space Nine* books. He lives in Los Angeles.

LAEL LITTKE lives in Pasadena, California, with six cats, two dogs, and a computer. She is the author of over thirty books for young people, and especially loves to write scary stories.

MICHAEL MARKIEWICZ has published several stories in this series. He has never seen a ghost, but while playing his guitar, he has seen other people turn white and run away in fear. Michael lives in Pennsylvania with his wife and their two beagles.

JESSICA AMANDA SALMONSON is a recipient of the World Fantasy, Lambda, and ReaderCon Awards. She's published a half-dozen novels and a gazillion short stories and poems, several in "year's best" anthologies. Her novelette "Namer of Beasts, Maker of Souls" was published in *The Merlin Chronicles.* She lives in Seattle.

NEAL SHUSTERMAN is the author of many award-winning novels, including *The Eyes of Kid Midas* (an ALA Best Book for Reluctant Readers) and *What Daddy Did* (an ALA Best Book). His short story collections include *Darkness Creeping* and *MindStorms.* He lives in Southern California with his wife, Elaine, and their two sons.

JOHN PIERARD, illustrator, lives with his dogs in a dark house at the northernmost tip of Manhattan. In addition to this series, he has illustrated the *My Teacher Is an Alien* quartet, the popular *My Babysitter Is a Vampire* series, and *Isaac Asimov's Science Fiction Magazine.*

Photo: Jules

BRUCE COVILLE was born and raised in a rural area of central New York, where he spent his youth dodging cows and chores, and letting his imagination get out of hand. He first fell under the spell of writing when he was in sixth grade and his teacher gave the class an extended period of time to work on a short story.

Sixteen years later—after stints as a toymaker, a gravedigger and an elementary school teacher—he published *The Foolish Giant,* a picture book illustrated by his wife and frequent collaborator, Katherine Coville. Since then Bruce has published over fifty books for young readers, including the popular *My Teacher Is an Alien* series. He has always had a special interest in ghost stories, and several of his books, including *The Ghost in the Third Row* and *Waiting Spirits,* feature ghostly themes.

These days Bruce and Katherine live in an old brick house in Syracuse with their youngest child, Adam; their cats Spike, Thunder, and Ozma; and the Mighty Thor, an exceedingly exuberant Norwegian elkhound.

The Yeerks Are Among Us.

ANIMORPHS™

Order your books...before it's too late!

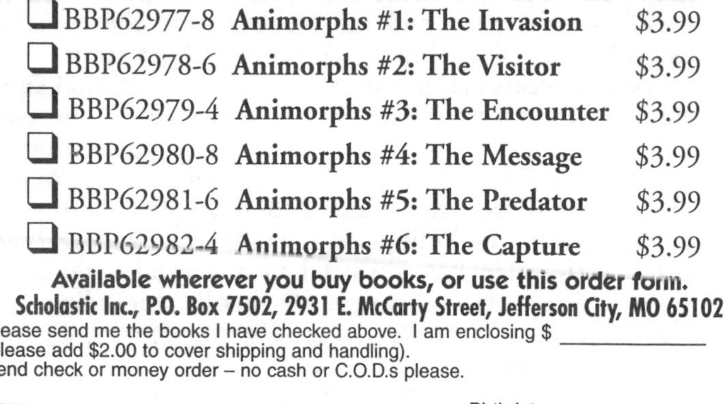

❑	BBP62977-8	**Animorphs #1: The Invasion**	$3.99
❑	BBP62978-6	**Animorphs #2: The Visitor**	$3.99
❑	BBP62979-4	**Animorphs #3: The Encounter**	$3.99
❑	BBP62980-8	**Animorphs #4: The Message**	$3.99
❑	BBP62981-6	**Animorphs #5: The Predator**	$3.99
❑	BBP62982-4	**Animorphs #6: The Capture**	$3.99

Available wherever you buy books, or use this order form.

Scholastic Inc., P.O. Box 7502, 2931 E. McCarty Street, Jefferson City, MO 65102

Please send me the books I have checked above. I am enclosing $ ____________
(please add $2.00 to cover shipping and handling).
Send check or money order – no cash or C.O.D.s please.

Name ______________________________ Birthdate ____________

Address ____

City ______________________ State /Zip ________________

Please allow four to six weeks for delivery. Offer good in U.S.A. only. Sorry, mail orders are not available to residents of Canada. Prices subject to change.

ANI796